# SAND AND SECRETS

KAYDENCE SNOW

Cover design by Sonder Publishing Pty Ltd

Editing by Kirstin Andrews

kaydencesnow.com

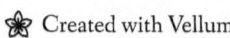 Created with Vellum

# CHAPTER ONE

The sunsets were always spectacular on Verbena Cove beach. The very air itself smelled different—warm and comforting and somehow sweeter—as the setting sun painted the sky in vivid colors.

It was the only time of day that I could forget why I was here.

For a few moments every evening, I could sit and marvel at the colors and the air and the sun as it took a lazy breath and dipped into the vast water. For a few moments, I could be just a girl, on a beach, watching the sunset.

The sand was warm under my palms, pleasant along the backs of my legs. It had been another hot summer day, and the sand would keep its heat for a few more hours at least. But the evening breeze was already starting to get a nip to it.

I drew my legs up and hugged my knees, putting off reaching for the hoodie in my backpack for just a little longer.

All around me, the beach crowd thinned as the sun drifted away, bidding the tourists and the locals alike a good evening. The surfers carried their boards in and headed for the outdoor showers near the parking area.

Only some teenagers and a few couples remained. And me, still watching the last little sliver of orange on the horizon, holding on to the illusion of serenity like the salty water held on to the sleepy sun.

"Hey, Chloe!" One of the girls I'd met a few weeks ago waved to me as she passed with a group of friends.

"Hey." I smiled and waved back.

She didn't stop to chat or invite me to join them. We hardly knew each other. We were just a couple of beach babes that happened to hang around the same beach most days.

My naturally dirty-blonde hair had been bleached by all the time in the sun, and my olive skin had darkened to a golden tan. With my bikini top and ripped-up jean shorts, my hair in messy beach waves—*actual* beach waves, not the ones I used to spend an hour in front of the mirror manufacturing with a straightener—I looked the part of the beach hippie. No one knew that I'd grown up hundreds of miles away from any beach and didn't know how to swim. I didn't even much like getting past my knees in the water, especially when the waves were high and the surfers swarmed the swell.

No one knew I was playing the longest game of pretend of my life, because no one really knew me here.

I made it a point not to get too close to anyone. I didn't want to get attached or have anyone start asking questions. I was here to find what I needed, and then I'd be gone.

The girl, Jess, and her friends continued past, taking their time up the sand and toward the only building on the strip of shops and cafés that still had its lights on.

Pelly's wasn't the only bar in Verbena Cove, but it was

the only one right on the beach. It was a café, restaurant, and night spot rolled into one, and it kind of worked, as establishments like this often did in small vacation towns. I didn't know how they survived during the winter without the tourists, but I wasn't planning to still be around to find out. Surely I'd find him by the end of summer.

It was fully dark by the time I hauled myself off the sand, pulled the hoodie over my head, and trudged toward the music and the lights and the smell of delicious greasy food.

I really wasn't in the mood for socializing, let alone for picking up a new guy, but I'd run out of money a week ago. The only way to avoid sleeping on the beach was to find a college guy living it up with his buddies and get an invite back to his hotel room for the night.

It wasn't something I was particularly proud of, but a girl had to do what she had to do. Besides, I didn't mind hanging out with people my age most nights, and I loved sex, so it wasn't like I was hating myself through it all. I'd done it three times already—three different guys, three different hotels. This system had the added benefit of getting me into hotels and parts of town I hadn't had a good excuse to be in before. Made it easier to search.

The crowd was decent tonight, the DJ playing a mixture of beach vibes dance tracks and reggaeton. There was sand all over the ground. Some people were finishing their dinner at the tables; some were hanging around the bar and the dance floor. Everyone was in shorts and tanks, ripped jeans, and loose sweatshirts. Half the girls still had bikini straps poking out of the tops of their hoodies.

A lot of people finished up their day at the beach by just heading over to Pelly's and partying the night away.

I made my way through the crowd slowly, doing my best

to look casual and friendly, looking for a group of guys. I just needed to make eye contact with one, and I'd have a beer and a bowl of fries within minutes.

My stomach growled. Jess had given me half her burrito when I bumped into her at the park around lunchtime. She'd sat down, and we chatted for a bit before she realized she was late to work, shoved the burrito at me, and ran off. She was a local and worked at one of the cute boutiques on the main street. I hadn't eaten anything since.

I steered clear of the bar as I walked toward the back of the room, where a few pool tables were set up. I wasn't doing anything illegal, but if the staff got suspicious . . . I wasn't sure what would happen exactly, but I couldn't risk anyone asking questions. Especially the locals.

My gaze locked with a guy in the corner. He was leaning on a pool cue, and he smiled when he saw me, standing up a little straighter. I smiled back. It had taken me only five minutes to find . . .

*Shit.* That was the guy from two nights ago.

I gave him a little wave and picked up my pace. There was a reason I didn't give them my number or talk about personal shit. No way could I risk a second night with someone.

Making my way to the wide-open front of the building —where tables and beanbag chairs spilled onto the beach under string lights—I decided to stay away from Pelly's for the night.

Resigned to sleeping on the beach, I managed to snag a half-empty basket of fries as I walked onto the sand, letting the darkness swallow me up.

Sometimes I wished it *would* swallow me up, for real. Sometimes I wanted to walk into a moonless night until my toes kissed the salty water and just keep going . . .

I walked to the rocky end of the beach, away from all the noise of the bar, and settled onto a flat rock to eat my cold fries.

I sat around for hours, just staring out at the pitch-black water and listening to the waves and far-off sounds of people getting drunk, having fun, living their best lives. There was no point trying to find a spot to sleep until Pelly's closed. And I couldn't even use my phone to distract myself. It had died earlier that afternoon, and I didn't want to walk all the way to the one gas station at the edge of town to charge it in the disgusting bathroom that had a convenient outlet.

So I stared out at the water, getting colder and hungrier and more uncomfortable as the hours passed.

It was well after midnight by the time they finally closed. I waited for the lights to go out and the sounds of staff calling goodnight to each other. Then I picked up my backpack and headed back in that direction.

There was a covered section that jutted out of the building, covering the sand. They never locked away the outdoor furniture. Who was going to steal solid wood tables and chairs? The beanbags were easy enough to carry around the corner where no one would see me from the parking lot, and they were pretty comfy once you got used to it.

I grabbed a pink one that didn't look as if it had been doused in beer and dragged it to my spot. The building provided shelter from the wind, and it was tucked away enough that I felt relatively safe. I'd be awake with the dawn and return the beanbag before even the surfers were out on their boards.

Tucking my hands into my sleeves, I shuffled around on the beanbag until I found a comfy position and immediately started to drift off. I was exhausted, and the rhythmic sound of the waves was like a lullaby.

I was just about asleep when the sound of footsteps crunching in the sand made me snap my eyes open. I held still and listened. It was probably just an insomniac going for a nighttime walk or something.

But the sound got closer, and then a tall, dark figure appeared from around the corner.

I startled, falling out of the beanbag, and somehow got tangled up in it while I shuffled back.

"Relax." The guy chuckled. His voice was deep but low, casual, as he sat down in the sand next to me, facing the water. I managed to extract myself from the beanbag's death grip and sit up a few feet away from him.

I cursed low under my breath when I realized he was one of the bartenders from Pelly's. I'd never spoken to him, but I'd noticed him. With that messy brown hair down to his chin, a deep tan, and a brilliant smile for every patron, how could I *not* notice him?

"Just relax," he told me for the second time, holding something out to me.

I instinctively leaned away. "Look, man, I was always going to return the beanbag, OK? I'll just put it back and be on my way."

"You're not in trouble." He chuckled again and shoved what I could now smell was a warm burger on a plate at me more forcefully. "Here. Eat."

I frowned at him. This was weird and suspicious. "I'm not hungry."

"Liar."

My stomach growled, siding with the beautiful bartender. Traitor.

With a sigh, I took the plate and started eating. The chicken burger was warm, tender, and juicy. I would've been happy with a cold, stale, dry one, but after I'd been starved for nearly twelve hours, this one was like heaven on a plate.

I couldn't help myself. I moaned.

He didn't make a sound, but I could see his shoulders shaking in silent laughter.

Whatever. I was going to wolf this thing down and get the hell out of here.

"So, what's your story?" he asked, leaning his arms on his knees, face still turned toward the water.

I was halfway through the burger, but I put it down on the plate and held it back out to him. "Thanks, but no thanks."

"What?" He whipped his head around and frowned at me.

"Look, I appreciate the gesture, but I'm not going to spill my guts for a burger, even if it is fucking delicious."

One corner of his lip twitched. He still wasn't taking the plate. "Just eat the damn burger. It's free. You don't have to tell me anything."

After a beat, I got back to eating. I was not in a position to turn down free food. And he got back to talking.

"I'm Riley. What's your name?" He smiled, as if we were a couple of normal people chatting on the beach. Except that it was the middle of the night, and nothing about this was normal.

"Come on." He smiled wider, amused. "I make you a fresh burger and personally deliver it, and you won't even tell me your name?"

"So the food's *not* free then." I managed to sound sarcastic even around a mouthful of burger.

He laughed and looked out at the water again, dropping it. I smiled despite myself.

"Chloe," I said after a long silence.

"Nice to meet you, Chloe."

I kept eating. I had nothing else to say to Riley, and I hoped he had nothing else to say to me.

"I've seen you around the past few weeks." No such luck. "Didn't think anything of it—lots of people vacation here. Until I noticed you've been sleeping on the beach."

I gave him a warning glare, and he held his hands up, leaning away.

"I'm not asking about it," he said. "I'm just offering you a place to stay. If you want it."

"What place?" I asked before I could stop myself. It would be nice to sleep through the night without random bartenders accosting me with free food.

"My place." He shrugged. "It's nothing special, but it's just up the beach there"— he pointed in the direction of the rocky end I'd just come from—"and the couch is pretty comfy."

I finished the burger and placed the plate on the sand between us.

"Nah, I'm good," I said as I stood. He wasn't asking questions now, but soon enough he'd want to know who the chick sleeping in his house was, what her story was.

"Wait." He scrambled to his feet as I grabbed my backpack. "Where are you going? I'm just trying to help."

"Thanks for the burger and the offer of your couch, but seriously, dude, I don't know you. No way in hell am I going back to your house in the middle of the night."

I took off, heading up the beach, away from where he said his house was. He followed, keeping pace.

"Where are you going to sleep?" he asked, sounding a little annoyed.

"What do you care?" I rounded on him. He was following me, and it was starting to freak me out.

"I'm just trying—"

"To help. Yeah, I got that. I'm telling you I don't want your help. Just back off, dude."

I turned and kept walking, glancing over my shoulder every few seconds. Thankfully, he didn't follow me, and eventually he walked off in the opposite direction.

No way would I be able to get to sleep with all this adrenaline coursing through me now—even if I did manage to find another safe spot.

Maybe I'd just sleep when I was dead.

## CHAPTER TWO

I spent the rest of the night in the park, jumping at every noise and hint of movement. That dick had put me on edge, and I was seeing and hearing danger everywhere. Verbena Cove was a quiet place. There were the locals who all seemed to know one another, the rich people who had vacation homes here, and the tourist crowd that cycled through the few hotels and resorts in the area. I hadn't even seen a homeless person, and I'd been sleeping on the beach for over a week now.

Oh god! Was that what I was now? Homeless?

Maybe, technically, but I knew I had an out as soon as I wanted it. I didn't want it—not until I found who I was looking for. He'd do the same for me.

My parents would have a fit if they knew their precious princess was sleeping on the streets. But they were the reason I had to, so they could go fuck themselves.

As the sun came up, I got to my feet and stretched my aching muscles. I'd spent the remaining few hours of darkness sitting at the base of the statue in the park. It was a concrete monstrosity, depicting a surfer on a board and an octopus on the other side of the same board—except that the surfer was on the underside, upside down. I was grateful that it was there, even if it was kind of weird. The solid stone had been comforting at my back when the rest of my surroundings felt so uncertain and disturbing.

I'd been close to tears several times, but I hadn't let myself cry. I'd wanted to give up, call my parents, but I hadn't. I'd just pressed my back harder against the stone and gritted my teeth through the few remaining hours of despair.

Once morning had dawned, it had banished all my weak thoughts along with the slight chill in the air.

I headed back to the beach as early as the surfers and set my towel up as they carried their boards into the water. Making sure I was in the shade of a tree at the back of the beach, I lay down and snoozed.

It was never proper sleep when you were in public, exposed, vulnerable. But I drifted in and out, comforted by the sound of other beachgoers and the knowledge that I looked like just another chick on vacay, lazing away the day.

No one disturbed me. No one even looked at me twice, but by midmorning it was impossible to sleep. The beach was packed with screaming kids running around, kicking up sand.

I sat up and ran my hands through my hair—or tried to. It was tangled as shit. And my mouth felt as if it was growing moss. It was time to take a walk to the gas station, freshen up, and charge my phone.

As I walked off the beach and turned my feet up the main road, I looked around at the sleepy town that was no longer sleeping. It was bustling with tourists and locals, people having brunch in the cafés or carrying floaties to the beach, just generally enjoying their lives on a perfect summer day.

I'd just crossed the street when a guy walked out of a café, his back turned to me. I froze, all the air leaving my lungs, as every other person around me faded into the background.

The blond hair cropped close to his head, the way he scrolled his phone with his left hand, his shoulders tilted just so.

"Ben," I breathed, feeling as though I might collapse right there in the street and cry.

"Ben!" I called and made my feet move.

I'd barely taken two steps when two other guys came running out of the café. They barreled into Ben, rough-housing as they laughed. Ben turned, shoving one of them in the shoulder and trying to smack his junk, and I got a look at his face and . . . it wasn't Ben.

Now that I could see him properly, I had no idea how I could've even thought that dude was my brother.

Ducking my head, I turned around and walked away with my arms wrapped around myself. I speed-walked to the gas station, focusing on the burn in my lungs and the sun on my back. Anything but the sting in my eyes.

The disabled bathroom at the back of the building was as gross as always, but it was empty. I slammed the door shut and turned the lock just as the first tear broke free. I growled, my jaw aching from how hard I gritted my teeth. For the first time since arriving in Verbena Bay, I let myself cry. I leaned against the filthy door of a gas station bathroom and let it see my frustration, my sadness, my despair.

I missed my brother. I just wanted to know he was OK. I was not leaving until I found him.

With that last thought, I pulled a deep breath into my lungs and pulled my shit together.

After freshening up as best I could in the small sink and letting my phone charge to half battery, I put my sunglasses on and walked back to town. I even spotted a five-dollar bill in the grass by the road. Maybe luck was on my side today after all. Maybe I would see Ben for real. Or that other guy in the photo.

Who would've thought that finding a fiver on the ground would lift my mood so much? Considering how much money I knew was in my bank account, it was preposterous.

I took the fiver to a fast-food place, got myself a coffee and a small breakfast roll, and sat at a table outside.

Having a full belly made me feel better too. *Hangry* was a legit emotion, and it was no joke. That made me think about the burger Riley had brought me the night before, so I focused on the coffee instead. It was pretty average, but I'd gone three days without caffeine, and it felt as if an angel was pouring pure light into my soul with every sip.

"Hey, girl." Jess sat down next to me, as though this was just part of our routine and we'd known each other forever. For the first time, it made me smile instead of making me mildly irritated. It was nice to see a friendly face after the night and morning I'd had.

"Hey, Jess." I gave her a genuine smile, sipped my coffee, and sighed.

"I *know* that coffee is not that good," she said, rummaging in her bag. "So, what's making you look so damn happy? You get some last night?"

She finally found what she was looking for, pulling a cigarette out of the pack and lighting it.

I snorted. "I wish. Just enjoying the peace for a few

moments." *And watching all the passing faces for ones I might recognize.*

"Got much on for the day?" She took a drag that looked as if it was giving her as much pleasure as the coffee had given me.

"This and that." I shrugged, keeping it vague. "You?"

"Work." She rolled her eyes and glared at the boutique across the street. "I start in fifteen."

"Gross."

"I know, right? Don't get me wrong—I'm happy to have a job until summer ends and I can go off to college—but my *god*, these tourists are so fucking rude sometimes. I mean . . ." She trailed off, cringing. "Sorry. I forget you're not a townie."

I waved her off and laughed. "I'm not exactly a vacationer either."

"True that." She cocked her head at me and took another drag. "Where did you come from, Chloe . . . er . . . what's your last name?"

"Hah! Nice try," I joked but kicked myself for letting the conversation turn to this topic. "I'm from a place far, far away. And I'm not leaving until I find what I came for."

*Why did I just say that?* What the hell was wrong with me?

"Ah." Jess nodded sagely. She finished off her smoke and put it out on my discarded wrapper. "A quest. Do tell."

"Where are you going to college?" I deflected.

"Fine. Keep your secrets." She glared at me but smiled.

We spent another ten minutes chatting, mostly about her and her plans after the summer. I learned that Jess had graduated a year earlier but hung around and worked because her dad had gotten in an accident and couldn't work until his shoulder healed. He was doing better though, so Jess was off to college in a few short months. On a scholarship, no less. She was smart and funny, and I could see us being real friends.

Hell, she'd been more of a friend to me in the past few weeks than my *actual* friends, who hadn't bothered to check in even though I hadn't spoken to anyone since I left. Assholes.

"Listen, I gotta get to work, but come to Pelly's tonight, OK?"

"I dunno. Maybe." I wasn't sure that was such a good idea just yet.

"Come on. There's someone I want you to meet. Dinner's on meee," she sang as she walked backward away from me.

I wasn't sure where my next meal was coming from, so that alone was tempting enough to get me to agree. This mysterious someone she wanted me to meet was suspicious, but I was pretty paranoid these days, and the more locals I could meet the better. One of them might just lead me to my brother.

"Fine." I rolled my eyes. "Go. You're already late."

"See ya tonight." She grinned and ran across the road.

I got back to watching the faces in the crowd.

# CHAPTER THREE

The sunset was painting the sky in the most wonderful warm colors, reflecting off the water as I sat on the sand.

My stomach growled. I hadn't eaten since that morning, and I'd spent the rest of the day hanging around the beach and the main street—the busiest parts of town.

"How'd I know I'd find you here?" Jess plopped down next to me.

"I guess I'm just predictable." I shrugged.

"Somehow, I think you're anything but."

We watched the pretty colors over the water for a few moments. Behind us, the string lights at Pelly's turned on, and the smell of their grill wafted down the beach, making my mouth water. It was fisherman's night. Once a week, they got a big haul of seafood from a local fisherman and sold it as menu specials, grilled right out on the sand in front of you.

"Chloe, I wanted to talk to you about something." Jess sounded a bit uncertain.

"Yeah? What's that?"

"I heard about what happened last night," she said gently.

I sighed and looked up to the darkening heavens.

"I didn't know you had nowhere to sleep. I'm really sorry—"

"Is that what this is?" I cut her off. "You're buying me dinner because you feel sorry for me? I don't need your pity."

"No. I genuinely like you as a person, and I'm just worried about you, OK? Stop being a dick."

To be fair, I was kind of being a dick. "I'm sorry. I just . . . I don't want to talk about it."

"Talk about what?"

"Any of it. Where I'm from. Why I'm here. Why I don't have any money." None that I was willing to touch anyway.

"That's cool." She shrugged. "I just wanna buy you dinner. Maybe even a beer. See if we can pick up a few rich boys on vacay."

Despite myself, I smiled. "How did you find out about last night?"

"Riley's a friend of mine. It's a small town."

"Great." I dug my heels into the sand. "He's going around talking shit about me."

"Not at all. He's just . . . never mind. Point is, he's a good guy. He shouldn't be, considering . . . but he is. He won't hurt you, if you choose to stay with him. He legit wants to help. I made some shitty choices last year when I had to put off college and all that. I did some really stupid shit, started to go down a bad path. Riley helped me. I just want you to know that you're not alone—not if you don't want to be. You have someplace to go, someone who genuinely cares."

"I'm not lost or in trouble or whatever," I tried to explain. "I'm just trying to . . . do something."

I raked my hands through my hair in frustration. She thought I was some runaway on a sure path to drug addiction and homelessness, but I couldn't tell her the truth.

"Can we just talk about something else?" I begged. "Who did you want to introduce me to?"

"Right. About that . . ." She cringed a little.

"Jess!" a male voice called from behind us, interrupting what she was about to say. We both turned to look. Three people were making their way over—a girl our age and two guys.

We got to our feet as they approached.

"Let's go eat. I'm starving!" the girl called out.

I didn't recognize one of the guys, but as they joined us, the other one was very familiar.

"This is who you wanted to introduce me to?" I turned an incredulous look on Jess. She had the decency to look guilty.

"I just thought if you guys could sit down again and talk . . ." She shrugged.

"Hey, Chloe." Riley gave me a tentative smile. "Come have dinner with us and—"

"No." I threw my backpack over my shoulder. "I'm not a troubled teen, I'm not a charity case, and I don't need your pity. Just fucking back off."

I stormed away from them, feeling angry and frustrated and so damn hungry.

I knew my reaction had been over-the-top, but I really hated being lied to. Especially by someone I was actually starting to trust.

I slept on the beach that night—the park end, away from Pelly's and the comfy beanbags. I was so exhausted from all the emotions of the last few days and not having eaten in so long that I actually managed to completely pass out. I didn't even wake up until midmorning when a couple of kids ran right past my head, kicking up sand.

I startled and sat up, looking around the busy beach. My stomach clenched, and my knees wobbled as I stood.

Walking all the way to the gas station was out of the question, so I just went to the public bathrooms and change-rooms at the back of Pelly's. I drank water straight from the tap until my stomach felt as if it was a giant sloshing water balloon.

The day was a blur.

I knew I needed to be on the main road, on the beach—that I needed to look at people. I was looking for Ben. But where was he?

Was I meeting him here?

Oh, that's right, he was missing.

I was *so* hungry. Or was I full? So full that I felt as if I might vomit?

Everything blurred together. At one point I found myself rummaging through my backpack, looking for the credit card I had stashed way at the bottom. I had to eat something. So what if the transaction showed where I was? I found the card and stumbled toward Pelly's.

Vaguely, I registered that the sun was setting, doing that pretty painting on the sky over the water bit. I frowned, wondering when it had gotten to evening.

What had I been doing all day?

I glanced down at the credit card clutched in my hand. I gasped and dropped it as if it had burned me.

What the hell was I thinking? I couldn't use that. Not until I found Ben.

But I *had* to eat. I was coherent enough to know that I

was bordering on dangerous territory if I didn't eat soon. I couldn't remember when I had water last either.

"Water," I murmured, determined to keep my shit together until I reached the building and the public toilets behind it.

I crouched down to pick up the credit card, and the sand suddenly started swirling around my head, as though a mini tornado had kicked up around me.

Next thing I knew, I was lying down in the sand, my face pressed into the gritty stuff, my shoulder hurting from where I'd fallen.

"Shit." I managed to push myself up into a sitting position and jammed the card back into my bag. I tried to get to my feet. I was on all fours when everything started to spin again, and I was falling.

Strong hands kept me from copping another face full of sand.

"I got you," a gentle male voice said as he righted me.

"Riley?" I squinted up at him. My vision was blurry, but I was pretty sure it was him.

"Yeah, it's me. It's Riley. Chloe, what happened?" His voice was sharper now, more urgent. His hand came up to my cheek, and he leaned in really close.

Was he about to kiss me? What the actual . . .

But he just looked into my eyes one by one as if he was searching for something.

"Chloe? Did you take something? Stay with me." He gave my cheek a gentle slap.

*That motherfucker*. I slapped his hand away, although I was so weak that it was more like half-cooked spaghetti sliding off the edge of a counter. "I'm not on drugs. I just need . . ."

Man, it was hard to keep my thoughts straight.

"What do you need? Focus, Chloe. Look at me."

"Water," I said, actually managing to focus my eyes long enough to meet his. "And food."

I dropped my head in embarrassment. That and I couldn't look into his eyes anymore. They were too knowing, too easy to get lost in.

"OK. Let's get you fed and watered then," he said as he readjusted his grip and picked me up in his arms.

"I'm not a horse," I complained.

He just chuckled, the rumble reverberating through his chest. I could feel it on my arm.

"I can walk. You don't need to carry me." I made a weak-ass attempt at wiggling out of his hold.

"Uh-huh. Sure." His grip tightened. "You couldn't even stand."

I was going to argue. I had a really great comeback too. But it felt kind of nice to be rocked, and I just laid my head on his shoulder and closed my eyes.

When I opened them again, I was no longer on the beach. I was in a softly lit room on a floral-patterned couch under a blanket. Music played in the background, and the smell of something delicious and fried wafted over to me from the small kitchen.

I pushed myself up onto my elbows, frowning. Where in the hell was I?

"Whoa. Hey, take it easy." Riley appeared out of a back room and leaned over me with concern in his eyes.

"What . . . where am I?" My voice sounded rough and croaky.

"At my place." He shoved a bottle of blue liquid at me, and I reflexively took it. "Drink that before you even think about standing."

He pointed a finger at me, rushed into the kitchen, and

cursed softly as he quickly did something at the stove, back turned to me.

"I told you I didn't want your help," I grumbled, opening the Gatorade and taking a long drink.

"Yeah, well, it was either leave you on the beach to die, take you to the hospital, or"—he turned to face me, spatula in one hand and a plate in the other—"bring you home. I figured you couldn't afford the medical bills, and leaving women for dead is not really my style, so here we are."

He gave me a wide grin. It seemed mostly genuine, but there was definitely a hint of snark in there too. As if he was daring me to argue. I wasn't going to. His logic was solid, and I was actually thankful. I was just confused more than anything.

Luckily, Riley was a chatty type and filled me in on everything without my having to ask.

"I carried you back to my place because it was the closest, and then I got you to drink most of a bottle of water, and you fell asleep." He brought two plates over, plonked himself on the couch at my feet, and handed me one.

Over grilled cheese sandwiches, he told me all about the embarrassing, incoherent things I'd said; told me I'd been asleep for about an hour; went into detail about his grilled cheese recipe when I made the mistake of saying it was good; and reassured me he hadn't done anything but tuck me in and rehydrate me.

I believed him. I didn't feel violated or afraid or any of the normal things you'd expect to feel after waking up in a stranger's house. I just felt warm and safe and full.

It's amazing the basic things we take for granted when we grow up financially secure.

During a rare lull in the—mostly one-sided—conversation, I cleared my throat and made myself look him in the eye. "Riley, thank you."

"You're welcome." He nodded, more serious now.

Then he got to his feet and pointed to a door next to the kitchen. "That's the front door, technically. Path leads to the road, but I really only use that door." He pointed to the sliding door on the opposite side of the room. It opened onto a deck, and the sound of waves could be heard through the screen door. The kitchen, the living room, and a small dining area were all in the one small room.

He pointed out the rest of his modest home. "That's the bathroom, and there's an outdoor shower through there as well. That other door is my room. You can have my bed for tonight, considering you nearly offed yourself with dehydration and heatstroke today, but if you're staying longer, we'll have to set the couch up or something. My back gets—"

"Riley." I cut him off, getting to my feet. Man, this dude liked to talk. "Why are you being so nice to me?"

I wasn't being rude or combative. I genuinely wanted to know. He and Jess had both gone out of their way to help me.

He sighed and looked toward the screen door and darkness beyond. "We all have stories we'd rather not tell. I know what it's like to feel like you have no choices. I'm just trying to give you choices." He shrugged, still staring out at the night.

We all had our demons. I guess once you'd wrestled with your own, it made it easier to recognize that fight in others.

I still didn't know this guy from a bar of soap, but his actions had been nothing but honorable so far, and I really did need someplace to stay. Plus, the chatty asshole might just tell me something useful. Something that could help me find my brother.

"I'll take the couch," I said.

"You sure?" He finally pulled himself out of whatever dark place he'd been visiting in his mind and looked at me.

"Yeah. Better get used to it if I'm going to be staying here for a while."

He flashed me a genuine smile. "OK. Actually, that's good. My room is a dump, and I haven't changed the sheets in a while."

"I'm sure it's more comfortable than a beanbag," I joked, and we shared a genuine moment of lightness. We already had inside jokes. This could work out just fine, as long as I didn't get too close.

The thought sobered me up.

"Riley, thank you so much. I mean it. You have no idea how much this means to me. But please know that there are things I'm not willing to talk about, so please don't try to get my sad story out of me, OK?"

"I'm not going to push you to tell me what your deal is, but you will. Eventually." He gave me a confident smile.

"As if I could get a word in," I teased. But that was what worried me the most—that I'd let my guard down without even realizing it and ruin my chances of ever seeing my brother again.

# CHAPTER FOUR

I awoke to the sound of waves crashing on the sand, as I had for days, but this time I was well rested and comfortable, and the sounds were accompanied by the smell of fresh coffee.

I stretched and made an obnoxious yawning sound.

Riley laughed, and I turned to see him leaning back against the kitchen counter, coffee in hand, eyes full of amusement.

"Sorry." I sat up, embarrassed. "Didn't realize you were there."

"Coffee?" He held the pot up.

"Yes, please." I sounded downright desperate.

He raised his eyebrows as he poured me a cup. "Really likes coffee. Got it."

"What, are you compiling a list about me?" I took the coffee and joined him at the counter.

"Something like that," he murmured, then downed the rest of his coffee and dropped the mug in the sink. "I gotta head off. Working the day shift at Pelly's today. There's food in the fridge. Make yourself at home."

He hardly gave me a chance to say "thanks" and "bye" before he disappeared out the door. I couldn't believe he was just trusting me in his house. I could steal all his shit while he was gone.

I looked around, taking the place in properly in the daylight. On second thought, there really wasn't anything worth stealing. It was my bitchy, privileged upbringing that caused that thought, but it was true.

He may not have had anything worth stealing, but I was sure Riley had some secrets buried in the privacy of his home. The urge to snoop was strong. I was curious about this gorgeous guy who lived on the beach and had a painful enough past and a big enough heart to help me.

But I was keeping my cards close to my chest and respected his right to do the same.

Instead, I made myself scrambled eggs and ate them out on the small porch overlooking the beach. The little cabin was the only building in sight, and I was pretty sure it was positioned on the other side of the rocks at the Pelly's end of the beach. He had his own little private beach back here, and it was gorgeous.

I was eager to get out there and look for Ben, but after a long, blissful shower, I spent some time cleaning. I washed Riley's sheets, tidied up, and did the pile of dishes in the sink. I couldn't pay him rent or anything like that, so this was the least I could do.

The rest of the day I spent searching for answers. I hung out at the beach and around town, popped into Jess's work to apologize for being a dick and to thank her. The whole time, I scanned the faces of everyone I passed, occasionally checking the photo on my phone of the guy with my brother. The guy I'd been warned against asking about.

When I kept coming up empty, I didn't feel so hopeless

and defeated. I was just ready to keep going the next day. Amazing what a difference a good night's sleep could make.

In the late afternoon, I found myself in the park, sitting on a bench. I wasn't obsessively scanning the faces of the people walking past. I was looking out at the pier and the approaching sunset, and I was drawing it.

I hadn't brought any of my art supplies, so I was working with a lined notepad and basic pencil, but it was feeding my soul all the same. I hadn't realized how much I'd missed drawing until I sat down and got the overwhelming urge to remember this moment, this view, this feeling that I couldn't quite name.

I did my best with what I had but gave up on it as the light started to disappear.

After watching the view for a while, I grabbed my phone and went into my voicemails, selecting the only saved recording. The electronic voice informed me that the message was recorded at 3:18 a.m. on a date several weeks ago. Then my brother's voice came on, and I found myself listening closely, as I always did, even though I'd heard it a million times.

"Hey, it's me." He sounded rushed and out of breath, his voice low but urgent. "I'm not sure why I'm even calling you. It's not like you can do anything from all the way over there. Not like I'd want to get you involved in this shit anyway." A pause, some rustling. "I fucked up, Chloe. I made some really bad choices and now . . . now I want to come home. I want to see you and tell you all about it and do something other than . . . Listen, I'll call you in the morning. But if I don't." There was a heavy pause, a loaded pause full of ominous silence. A bird called in the distance. Then Ben's voice came through the phone again, even quieter, almost a whisper. "If I don't, I'm stashing it at hengeit under the tunas."

The line went dead, and I squeezed my eyes shut, remembering how confused I'd been when I first listened to the message. I'd tried calling him several times that day, but it always went right to voicemail.

What did it mean? What was he doing when he called me at such an ungodly hour with a cryptic message? I knew my brother. We were only a year and a month apart, and we were close. He didn't sound as if he was high. He was trying to tell me something. Just me. No one else had received a call or a message from him.

Every time I listened to it, I felt awful for not being able to figure out what he was trying to tell me. I had no idea what "hengeit" was even supposed to mean, even after trying to google it, and how the hell do you put something under a tuna?

My phone vibrated in my hand, startling me.

I groaned but answered it anyway. "Hey, Mom."

"Hello, Chloe, darling." She sounded positively chipper. Not at all as if her son was missing. "How are you?"

"I'm fine. How are you, Mom?"

"Very busy but doing great. Missing my daughter." She babbled on about work and her social engagements and the vacation in Europe she and Dad were planning, before adding in a guilt trip. "Are you sure you wouldn't like to come with us? We can go to that little place you love in Venice. We haven't seen you since Christmas, darling, and I positively can't stand not seeing you all summer. What are you even doing with all your time?"

*Looking for my brother. Your son. Remember him?* I swallowed down what I really wanted to say and gave her a

28

vague response about other commitments and volunteering for extra credit.

When I'd gotten the disturbing voicemail from Ben, my parents didn't seem worried at all. They hadn't spoken to him in months, but they chalked it up to "just more of his dramatics" and said they "didn't want to indulge his attention-seeking behavior." Even when he hadn't been in contact with anyone for over a week, they didn't give a shit. I had to go to the police myself and report him as missing —or try.

The police refused to do anything. He'd quit college during his senior year, had a massive falling out with my parents—because he was no longer willing to contort himself into the mold they demanded he fit into—packed up his stuff, and left. He spent some time traveling with friends, had a few odd jobs here and there. He was finding himself, and I was so proud of him for following his heart. I wished I had the strength to do what he'd done. To be who I really was deep down inside. But I wasn't prepared for that battle with my parents, or myself, so I'd stayed at college, doing my marketing degree and hanging out with my friends who didn't really know me.

Ben had kept in touch. We'd spoken nearly every day. Until that voicemail.

The police said they'd look into it, but after a week, I had to pester them for information, and they finally told me they'd spoken to my parents and a few of his friends. He'd stopped speaking to all of them, and they believed I was the last person he'd decided to cut ties with. The voicemail didn't contain anything worrying as far as they were concerned. They weren't treating it as suspicious at all.

I was beyond pissed. I knew my brother. He would never just abandon me like that. And I wasn't going to abandon him either. If no one else was going to look for him, if no one else was going to care, I sure as hell would.

So I packed a bag, took a cash withdrawal from Daddy's credit card, and got my ass to Verbena Cove. That was the last place he'd been. He'd sent me photos of the beautiful beach and talked about what a nice little town it was. The only other photo was of him and a guy he'd met there, the two of them on the beach, smiling at the camera with sunglasses on.

This town and that person were the only leads I had.

"And what have you been doing with your free time?" Mom asked, poorly hiding what she really wanted to know.

*Looking for your son, sleeping on the beach, and starving half to death.* "Just regular stuff. Hanging with my friends and whatever."

"Oh, OK. That's good, honey. And do you need any money?"

"Nope." I smiled to myself. I'd lost a lot of respect for my parents recently, and it was easier to mess with them now.

"Right . . . because your father says you haven't really used the credit card recently, so we just wanted to make sure."

There it was. They hadn't been able to keep tabs on me through my transactions, and it was killing them.

It nearly killed me too. That's why I refused to use the card in my bag. My parents would find out where I was and come here to drag me home.

"Haven't needed it," I said, keeping my voice casual. If she wanted to know things about my life she had no business knowing, she was just going to have to ask the intrusive questions.

"Chloe—"

"Hey, Mom, I gotta go. Nina and I are about to head out. I'll talk to you later." I hung up, not willing to entertain that reproachful tone that had entered her voice.

I ground my teeth and closed my eyes as I took a deep, cleansing breath.

"Hey, stranger." Riley's voice made me open them again. He sat down next to me, one ankle crossed over the opposite knee.

"Hey." I gave him a tight smile, the tension from my phone call still lingering.

"Oh, wow!" He pulled the notebook I'd forgotten about out of my lap and held it up. "That's pretty good."

"I don't have the right tools and the paper is lined . . ." I ducked my head. "Thanks."

He handed the notebook back and stood. "You busy? Wanna come have dinner with me and Ziggy?"

"What's a Ziggy?"

"You kind of have to meet Ziggy to really understand the Ziggy. And since you're an artist, I want to show you something."

I was already living with the guy, so what the hell.

"Lead the way." I got to my feet, ignoring a second call, from my dad this time.

# CHAPTER FIVE

R iley led me past the main street and through a residential area. As we walked, he pointed out things about the town—the spot where he fell off his skateboard at age twelve and cracked his head open, the house where his first girlfriend used to live, and the secret passageway between two houses that led to a field where kids hung out doing shit they weren't supposed to.

It was barely a fifteen-minute walk before the houses thinned out and we turned into a more industrial-looking area—or as industrial as it got in a small coastal town. There were a few older houses about, but there was also a lumber-yard, a mechanic, a few other businesses with faded signs, and flickering streetlights.

We headed for a low building without any signage, and Riley opened a side door next to the big roll-up garage door.

I eyed him warily, then peeked at the absolute dark-ness inside. The area was deserted, and I hardly knew this guy.

He laughed. "So, you do still have a sense of self-preservation."

"Yeah, and if you do as well, you'll stop testing mine." I crossed my arms over my chest.

"That you, kid?" a gravelly male voice called from inside. Lights started to come on, and a shriveled old man appeared at the door. "Who's this?"

He was skinny, and he had white hair down to his shoulders and a beard to match. His skin had that leathery-brown quality that came from a lifetime spent in the sun—before we knew the importance of sunblock. He looked like a surfer who had been left out in the sun to dry—for forty years.

"This is Chloe. Chloe, meet Ziggy." Riley pushed past Ziggy and into the building. The old man grunted in my general direction, and we followed Riley into . . . uh . . . I had no idea what this place was, actually.

There were several metal benches; a bunch of wooden implements, some of them in water barrels; and torture-device-looking metal tools. Several large ovens also lined the back wall. I knew they were ovens only because one of them was radiating white heat through the round opening in the front.

Riley opened the roller door—an old, manually-operated one that sounded as if it was just as likely to fall apart as open—then came over to me.

"Have you ever worked with glass?" he asked as we watched Ziggy fiddle with some of the metal torture devices.

"What?" I frowned at Riley.

"As an art form. This is a glassblowing workshop—a hot shop. Ziggy over there might look like a hippie and a sultana had a baby, but he's the best glass artist on the coast."

"You're an artist, sweet thing?" Ziggy's sullen mood dropped, and he was all smiles suddenly.

After that, it was as if I was a part of their weird little family. The old man was almost as chatty as Riley. We had pizza delivered, Ziggy pulled beer out of a little fridge next to the dilapidated couch in a corner, and we sat around drinking, eating, and chatting.

I answered a few questions about my art, but other than that, the two of them did all the talking.

They'd both been born and raised in Verbena Cove but had only struck up an unlikely friendship in the past few years. There were a few vague hints at Riley's shady past, but I didn't want to pry. If I started asking personal questions, so would he. My curiosity would just have to burn like the furnace and the glory hole. Yes, they'd also taught me what some of the key equipment in the hot shop was, and yes, its actual real name was "glory hole."

Ziggy had been teaching Riley his craft, and they'd bonded over it. Riley had found a passion in glass, but there wasn't exactly a massive demand for handblown glass artists, so he worked at Pelly's as well.

"All right. I'll leave you kids to it." Ziggy hauled himself to his feet and let out a racking cough. "Lock up when you leave."

He waved goodbye and walked out through the wide-open roller door.

It was a mild night, but the glory holes had openings in the front, and they were keeping the hot shop . . . well, *hot*.

"Wanna help me make a paperweight?" Riley flashed me a grin, clearing the empty pizza boxes and beer cans into the trash.

"I have no idea what I'm doing." I laughed.

"Neither did I. I'll teach you."

He took his shirt off and started gathering supplies. He

had a defined back, a narrow waist. Had he always had such a tight ass? How had I not noticed that?

"So is taking my shirt off the first part or . . ." I teased.

He gave me a sly look over his shoulder. "Strictly speaking, no, it's not. But it's only going to get hotter in here, and I won't complain if you want to get naked."

"Yeah, I bet."

He ran me through the basics of safety around fire and extreme heat. Then he explained everything he was doing as he went, putting as much detail into it as he always did when talking about anything.

Heat blasted me in the face when he opened the furnace to gather the molten glass with a blowpipe, but I didn't even care. I was fascinated with the process, and Riley's passion for the craft was infectious.

He was a patient man, explaining things to me in a gentle, calm voice, correcting my grip on the blowpipe with soft touches as he let me blow air into the cooling glass while he shaped it. I was mesmerized by it all—the excitement of learning something new, the inherent danger that was part of the process, and spending time in Riley's presence.

There was something about him. He was rough around the edges, but he had an innate ability to make those around him feel safe and comfortable.

Not to mention the fact he remained shirtless.

It got hotter and hotter as we worked. My muscles burned from being used in new ways, and my skin burned from being so close to the intense heat. Something else burned too—something deep inside of me that was harder to label.

And the sweat glistening on Riley's chest and arms only seemed to stoke that indescribable heat.

With his shorts slung low on his hips and the fire casting shadows on his body as his muscles danced in the heat and the artistry—he was a vision. I wanted to draw him. I wanted to get back to learning how to work with oil paints so I could paint him and do the depth of the image justice.

But I didn't have any supplies, so I'd have to settle for watching him and committing the image to my mind.

By the end of the process, we'd made a paperweight larger than my fist. We'd used layers of blue and white glass, and Riley had shaped it before coating the whole thing in clear glass and making it perfectly round with a flat bottom. It looked like splashing waves and seafoam, frozen in time and caught in my hand.

Not that I was holding it just yet. Apparently, it had to go into the kiln to cool over the next twenty-four hours so it wouldn't crack.

I helped him clean up, and we chatted as we finished off a few more beers before leaving.

The sound of the roller door screeching closed was obnoxiously loud in the silent night. And it made us giggle like teenagers. The beer was making me feel light and free. Or maybe that was the company.

We walked back the way we'd come, cracking jokes and talking about art and glassblowing. A very surly middle-aged woman even came out onto her porch and yelled at us to "Shut up! People are trying to sleep!" as we passed through a residential street. Several dogs in the neighborhood started barking, and Riley and I laughed harder, breaking into a jog until we were safely around the corner.

As we ran away from the scary lady, I realized we were holding hands. And it kind of felt natural. My hand fit into his larger one, our sweat mingling. We were both drenched after a few hours in that heat, and Riley still had his shirt off.

I wasn't sure if he was as hyperaware of where our hands touched, but as we approached the beach, the chatter and laughing gave way to silence between us.

The gently rolling waves welcomed us as our feet crunched on the sand. Pelly's was pumping, the music and the lights bright, but it was background noise in the distance.

"Let's have a dip." Riley dropped my hand and marched toward the water. He toed off his shoes, dropped his T-shirt and then his shorts, and waded into the water in only his underwear.

"What are you doing?" I rushed to catch up with him but hesitated. I wasn't confident around water on a good day. At night, it was downright terrifying. *Anything* could be under the surface.

He looked over his shoulder and held his hand out. "Come on. It's rarely this still here, and the temperature is amazing. Trust me."

Weirdly, I did. And the water was incredibly still. This was a surf beach, and usually the waves were intense, energetically cresting over screaming kids.

Tonight, it was like ink, washing over the sand with soft strokes yet leaving no mark.

Without thinking about it too much—thank you, beer—I pulled my tank and shorts off, stepped out of my flip-flops, and followed Riley into the water in my bra and underwear.

I took his hand, and we waded in until we were waist deep. He was right about the water too—it was the perfect temperature, refreshingly cool after the heat of the workshop yet warm enough to feel like a soft caress in the night.

Keeping hold of my hand, Riley leaned back and let

himself fall gracefully under the surface. He emerged dripping wet, hair slicked back, and sighing as if it was the greatest pleasure in the world.

His skin glistened in the moonlight. I wanted to run my fingers over the curve of his shoulder so badly that my fingers actually twitched.

"Come on. It's really refreshing." He tugged on my hand.

I eyed the water warily. "I'm not really a water type of person. It's wigging me out that I can't see the bottom."

"I was not expecting that." He laughed softly. "For someone who spends so much time at the beach . . ."

I rolled my eyes. Now wasn't the time to talk about all that—or even worry about avoiding talking about it. For the first time in what felt like a hundred years, I was having fun.

Heart hammering for multiple reasons, I squeezed my eyes shut, took a deep breath, and fell back like Riley had. I kept a death grip on his hand, and he held it steady, my tether to safety as I submerged myself in the embrace of the silky water. The sounds fell away, and I felt a profound sense of peace.

It was fleeting, because I ran out of air and had to stand back up again, but I was grinning wide when I did.

Riley grinned right back at me. Then the asshole dropped my hand and splashed me, making me gasp. My heart started hammering again as mirth bubbled up in my chest, and I splashed him right back.

We chased each other, playing in the night-kissed water, diving and jumping and circling until we naturally started to slow our movements. We were slightly crouched, our arms treading water that was around our shoulders, as we panted and just . . . stared at each other.

A strand of hair was plastered to his cheek, and I

reached out and smoothed it back. He moved in closer, his fingers brushing against my waist in the water. The moon-light felt magical, the air between us electric, the water tugging us closer to one another.

I gave in to the urge I'd had all evening and caressed his shoulders, my fingers gliding over smooth skin and strong muscle.

His hand moved back to my waist, his touch firmer now, less uncertain. His other hand went to the sensitive spot at the side of my neck, and then we were nose to nose, belly to belly, our legs tangling in the water.

Our lips met in a gentle, moon-kissed embrace. And that was the last soft, gentle moment of the night. We were in water, but we'd come from fire, and I felt as though I was burning up from the inside again.

His tongue pushed into my mouth, claiming it, and I pressed myself against him harder, my arms wrapping around his neck.

I pulled away only when I realized I couldn't reach the bottom anymore. I gasped, multiple sensations coursing through my body. The desire mixed with the sudden flash of fear.

"I'm not a good swimmer," I said, water up to my chin.

"It's OK." His arms wrapped around me tighter, lifting me higher. "I've got you. I can still reach the bottom."

The feel of his body slick between my legs was intoxi-cating. I wanted to push his briefs down and lower myself onto his hard length, let my head go under. I was willing to sacrifice air for what I was pretty sure would be mind-blowing dick.

But I also didn't want to drown. I glanced at the beach, then back at his lips.

Riley chuckled and licked the side of my neck.

"How about we get you out of these wet clothes and continue this on dry land?" he said against my skin before sucking lightly on the same spot.

I shuddered, my hips rocking involuntarily.

"I'll take that as a yes," he said, slowly walking us back to shore.

"Yes," I breathed, kissing him deeply.

When the water was lapping at my hips, I pulled away and dropped to my feet. Riley tried to grab for me, but I turned and ran for the sand as fast as I could. He gave chase, and I let out a high-pitched sound, pumping my legs harder.

It was no use. He was taller and stronger, and he caught me quickly. He picked me up and swung me over his shoulder.

"There's no running away now," he teased, a playful growl riding his voice. Then he smacked my ass.

"Ah!" My yell was part outrage, part pure arousal. Riley groaned and picked up his pace. He set me down on the sand, and we collected our clothing, not bothering to put it all back on.

We half walked, half jogged up the beach, holding hands, exchanging heated looks. There was no more talking. We both knew it was on as soon as we got back to his place, and we were impatient to get there.

The music and voices coming from Pelly's got louder and then faded out again as we rushed past. At the rocky end of the beach, Riley led me back into the water and maneuvered us between the rocks, through a sandy path to the other side.

His place came into view, the porch peeking out from between the vegetation. I dropped my stuff and rushed ahead, unhooking my bra and discarding it as I went. His footsteps sped up, keeping pace. We pounded up the few steps onto the porch, and then his arm wrapped around me and pulled me flush against his chest as he walked us forward. I braced my hands against the door as Riley caressed my body with his, his mouth back on my neck.

I moaned as he palmed my breasts and ground his hips against my ass.

He dragged one hand down my front and all the way between my legs. His strong, sure fingers rubbed me over my wet underwear, and I ground myself against him unashamedly.

I wanted the release, I wanted the pleasure, I wanted to feel his skin on me, *in me*.

I reached down and pushed my panties off. The soaked material slapped onto the boards around my ankles, but Riley's hand didn't go back to its spot.

He turned me to face him, took my face in his hands, and looked me in the eyes. "Are you sure you want this, Chloe?" he panted inches from my face.

"Yes," I hissed and tried to pull him close once more, but he held me back.

"I don't want you to feel like you have to."

"What?" I frowned.

"I mean, you can stay with me even if you don't want to . . . There's no obligation. And you've been drinking."

This sweet idiot of a man.

"You've been drinking too. Neither one of us is too drunk to make adult decisions." I gripped his hand and guided it to between my legs. "And I'm not whoring myself out to you for room and board. Do I feel like I'm doing this out of obligation?"

His eyes fluttered closed as his hand glided through my slick folds. He pushed one finger in, my body welcoming the intrusion with more heat and arousal.

"Fuck," he breathed against my lips. "I want to feel you from the inside."

"Then I hope you have condoms, because I haven't been taking my pill."

He withdrew his finger, making me whimper, and rushed past me into the house. I stood on the porch in the dark, completely naked and stunned.

What the fuck?

Was a condom that much of a deal breaker? This motherfu—

The screen door banged against the side of the house as Riley rushed back out. He'd ditched his briefs and was rolling a condom down his thick length.

I couldn't help the hungry smile that took over my face at the sight of him. He was all man, his hair still damp, his body strong and sculpted, his cock so hard it was pointing up.

"Are you gonna ride it or eat it?" he said in that low, rough voice. "Because that's the same look you gave that burger I brought you."

I laughed, but I was beyond words, so I just showed him I was planning to ride it. Maybe I'd eat it later, but for now, I pushed him backward and to the side until he sat in the Adirondack chair. I didn't waste any time straddling him, and he held his cock at the base for me as I lowered myself onto it.

With a guttural groan, I impaled myself until he was all the way in, stretching me, filling me, reaching a place in my soul and not just my body.

With the moon shining down on us, I started to move, first up and down, learning the feel of him, the size of him. Then I took him in deep and sat up, moaning as the new angle hit a new spot.

He watched me with his mouth hanging open, his tongue darting out to lick his bottom lip from time to time. His hands kneaded my tits, fingers playing with my nipples, as his hips gyrated in rhythm with my pace.

This was my favorite position, especially when the guy knew how to move with me. I liked it deep and intense, and this position allowed me to grind my clit against his pelvis too. I could already feel my climax climbing.

The chair made short scraping noises as I fucked him harder, the sound mingling with our moans and grunts.

Riley alternated between playing with my breasts, gripping my hips, and smacking my ass. *Fuck*, but he was good at this. Sex was all relative. Different people liked different things. But Riley and I seemed to fit. We matched in the most delicious, depraved way.

"Oh, god." I threw my head back, eyes closed, hands threading into my messy hair as my movements became more choppy, more desperate.

Riley kept his pace steady, doing exactly what I needed to get there.

I yelled incoherent sounds into the starlit sky as I came. The heavens were above me, and ecstasy was under me.

My whole body tingled as wave after wave of pleasure washed through me. My core felt as if it was on fire, pulsating heat as the orgasm rocked through me.

With a gorgeous man under me, a blanket of stars above, and the wind caressing my sensitive skin, I felt like a fucking goddess.

I collapsed onto Riley's chest, spent, panting, my eyes wide with shock. That was the best orgasm I'd ever had with another person.

"You are a sight to behold when you come." He groaned, his length still thick and hard inside me.

I smiled against his chest and gave him a light bite. He yelped, but then he sprang into movement, sitting up and getting to his feet with me still on his dick.

He carried me to the porch rail and perched my ass on it. I tightened my legs and arms around him. That thing was flimsy as shit, and I did not want to break an arm or the rail itself.

"I got you. Relax," he said, one arm wrapping around my waist as the other pushed my thigh, opening me to him.

He'd said that several times in the last few hours—*I've got you*. I wasn't sure if he was doing it on purpose, but I was starting to believe him.

He didn't wait to make sure I heard him though, too far gone into the sex haze. Staring at where we were joined, his forehead against mine, he started pumping into me. He set a fast, punishing pace, slamming in and out, our skin slapping as he moaned loudly.

God, I loved it when men moaned and groaned and let loose their pleasure. It was such a turn-on. I felt another orgasm building. He was fucking me just how I liked it, and I couldn't get enough.

I clawed at his back, chasing that feeling, but he slammed into me with force as his body went taut, and he came, shuddering and moaning even as he kissed me. The sloppy, panting kiss turned into something more gentle, languorous, and he held me close and started to caress my back.

The rail was digging into my ass painfully, but I laid my head on his shoulder and stayed put. I liked it right where I was, right where he had me.

# CHAPTER SIX

J ust as I finished wiping down a table, the table of people next to it got up and left, so I quickly cleared the plates and cups from that one too and gave it a wipe down.

It was my second shift at Pelly's, and my arms and legs were still sore from the first shift. On top of that, my feet were killing me. I'd never worked this hard in my life—if I was being totally honest, I'd never actually worked—but I was no longer stuck between starvation and using the credit card my parents used to spy on me.

It had been just over a week since Riley and I had taken a midnight dip and then had the best sex of our lives. I wasn't assuming things. He'd told me as much the next morning after he took me from behind—the third time in under twelve hours.

We'd been all over each other ever since, fucking like rabbits every day, often more than once. I loved sex, but I'd never been this insatiable for it before. I craved his body, his hands, his mouth, as if it were my own customized brand of crack.

I deposited the tub of dirty dishes in the kitchen and wiped sweat off my brow with the back of my arm. It was a stinking-hot day, and the lunch crowd was downing beers as if they were water.

As I headed back out to clear more tables, Riley flashed me a grin from behind the bar, where he was pouring a beer. He'd gotten me the job when one of the busboys quit suddenly.

At first, I'd been worried I wouldn't have enough time to look for Ben, but I couldn't just mooch off Riley indefinitely. I needed to fund my own missing-persons search. Plus, I'd been trying to find Ben in the crowd for weeks already. Working at Pelly's would let me come into contact with more people, listen in on more conversations.

I worked hard for several hours, but the midafternoon brought a lull in the crowds, and the manager started sending staff out on our breaks. Riley had pestered me to wear my bikini under my shorts and Pelly's T-shirt when we left for work, and now I really understood why.

As soon as my break started, I marched down the hot sand, past the scores of vacationers and bright beach towels, and headed right for the water. I peeled my sweaty clothes off and launched my body under a cresting wave.

I'd gotten over my fear of water after spending so much time with Riley. If he wasn't at work or in the hot shop, he was in the water. Swimming, splashing around, dragging me in there. We'd even had sex in the salty, gentle waves. He'd pushed me up against a smooth rock near his house, pulled my bikini to the side, and fucked me in rhythm to the waves washing over us.

As I came out of the water, refreshed and ready for a meal—another bonus of working at Pelly's was the free staff meals—Jess came walking up.

"Hey, girl!" She pulled me in for a hug, and I returned it. Her skin was hot to the touch, especially compared to my cool just-dunked body.

"Hey, not working today?" I asked.

"Nah. Need to cool down. Our AC crapped itself again."

"The water's amazing." I grabbed my clothes and shook the sand out of them.

"Oh, how's your second day going?" she asked, pointing to my staff shirt.

"I'm sore in places I didn't even know I had." I gave her a wide, tight smile, and she laughed.

"Working hard then."

"Yeah, and I've built up an appetite. I'm gonna go eat before my break's over. Wanna join?"

She looked longingly at the water, then looped her arm through mine. "OK, fine, but I'm stealing your fries."

"Deal!" I laughed and pulled on my shorts. The baking sun had dried the sweat off my T-shirt, but I wasn't ready to put it back on just yet. Most of the customers at Pelly's wandered in in swimwear, fresh from the beach, anyway.

Jess and I chatted as we walked, making plans for drinks and pizza on the beach after Riley and I finished our shift.

It was a little crazy how quickly she'd become my friend, how quickly I'd settled into whatever this between me and Riley. We weren't talking about labels, but he hadn't asked me to move out of his bed, let alone his house, and I was more than happy to stay put.

I hadn't given up looking for Ben, not by a long shot, but the burden and heavy emotion that came with it was a little lighter. I still hadn't told Jess or Riley anything about it or my life back home, but I was seriously considering it. They were genuine and warm and made me feel as though I belonged here with them, bussing tables and diving into waves and ignoring calls from my parents.

Jess and I sat on stools at the bar, and Riley poured us some house-made lemonade and brought me a burger with fries. He occasionally served a drink to a customer but leaned on the bar and chatted with us in between.

Riley was in the middle of telling an embarrassing story about Jess from when she just started high school, when he stopped midsentence and stood to his full height, his eyes fixed on something behind us.

Jess turned to look a second before I did.

"Seth!" She jumped up to rush over to a guy and give him a hug, obscuring my view of his face.

Riley walked out from around the bar and stood next to me.

The hug ended, the new guy turned toward us, and all the air left my lungs.

The smile, the hair, he was even wearing the sunglasses from the picture.

Riley reached out and man-hugged the guy from the last picture my brother sent me—the face I'd been searching for in the crowd along with Ben's all this time.

The guy took those sunglasses off and looked right at me.

"And who's this?" He glanced between Riley and Jess before bringing his attention back to me.

It took everything I had not to let the storm of emotions show on my face. I forced myself to smile back and get off the stool.

Riley wrapped a casual arm around my neck. "Seth, this is Chloe. Chloe, meet my little brother."

# CHAPTER SEVEN

I started to reach out to shake Seth's hand, but I realized my own was trembling and gave him an awkward wave instead. "Nice to meet you."

"Where'd you come from, pretty lady?" Seth asked. He took my seat, helped himself to the last of my fries, and leaned back against the bar casually.

"No one really knows." Jess looked off to the side, eyes squinted, as if she was musing about some great mystery.

"I'd better get back to work," I said, collecting my shirt and turning away. I couldn't take another second of this.

"You've still got ten minutes!" Riley called after me.

"I need to go to the bathroom." I waved him off without turning around and actually headed to the staff bathroom.

I locked the door and leaned back against it, finally letting my face crumple and show all the emotion coursing through me.

"What the fuck?" I whispered into the empty space, wishing I could scream it. "What the *actual* fuck? *Why?*" I whined, sliding down the door. I stopped myself before I hit the floor. I really didn't have time to fall apart just yet.

I'd wanted to pounce on the guy my brother had called a friend and demand he tell me all he knew. I wanted to run out there and stick to him like a barnacle so he wouldn't disappear again, taking all my answers with him.

But I was still reeling from the fact that he was Riley's brother. What were the chances?

Riley had never mentioned a brother or anything much about his family at all, considering how much he liked to talk. I hadn't said shit about my family either, so I couldn't really blame him.

I had to be careful about how I handled this—least of all because the guy who could help me find Ben was the brother of the guy I was sleeping with.

My first day in Verbena Cove, I'd settled into my motel room, grabbed my phone and purse, and headed straight for the beach. I felt awkward at first, but my determination made me push through it. I approached total strangers and showed them the photo of Ben and Seth, asking them if they knew the men or had seen them around.

I'd gotten through maybe a dozen people, all of them completely clueless, when I walked up to a group of people my age. Most of them got up as I approached and headed into the water, but one girl stayed behind, working on her tan.

I crouched down next to her. "I'm sorry to bother you, but do you mind taking a look at this photo? Do you know either of the men in it? The one—"

"Put that away," she hissed at me, looking around, before I could finish what I was saying. "I don't know who you are or what your game is, but do yourself a favor and stay away from them."

"Who?" I frowned. It was a pretty extreme reaction.

"The guys in that picture, and others." She looked at me

properly, taking in my baffled expression. "You look like you legit don't know you were about to be in a world of trouble, so I'll do you a solid and not tell anyone about this, but seriously, you need to get lost. Do not go around this town asking people about that picture. You're bound to ask the wrong person eventually. Whatever it is you're trying to do, it's not worth it. Trust me."

Without another word, she'd gotten to her feet and gone off to join her friends, leaving me crouched in the sand, more confused than ever and now scared on top of it.

What the hell had Ben gotten himself into?

I splashed some water on my face, then leaned on the sink and stared myself down in the mirror. This was the first hint of solving the mystery of Ben's whereabouts I'd had since I got here. I could not afford to fuck this up. Seth was clearly into some shady shit, and I couldn't spook him.

First things first—I had to get through the rest of my shift as if there was nothing wrong. I'd figure out my next steps after.

I pulled my T-shirt back on, retied my damp hair, and headed back out there.

Jess was gone, but Seth was still at the bar with Riley. They were leaning in close, talking quietly. Riley seemed uneasy, the muscles in his arms and shoulders taut. I went to a table nearby and took my time clearing it, trying not to look as though I was watching them. There was too much noise to hear what they were talking about, but I was close enough to see the tense looks on both their faces.

Seth said something that made Riley narrow his eyes and grit his teeth, then Seth got up and walked out. Riley smacked the bar top and stormed into the storage room. I burned to know what they were arguing about, but I kept my head down and worked.

The dinner rush was busier than the lunch rush, and I hardly saw Riley until we both finished our shifts. The kitchen had stopped serving food, and the party crowd was rolling in.

I was dismissed first, and I waited for him on the beach, looking out over the water. The waves looked higher under the cloudy sky, more tumultuous and forceful.

Riley appeared next to me and took my hand.

"Ready?" he asked, looking at the waves too.

I nodded, and we headed back to his place, our feet in the water as it rolled over our ankles.

He didn't speak the entire way. I'd never seen him this quiet. It was unsettling.

When we reached the porch, he dropped my hand and walked through the bathroom to the outdoor shower, where he stayed for a long time. I changed into a dress, made myself and him a sandwich, and tidied up. I was tired, but I couldn't sit still. Not after the bombshells of the past few hours. Not when Riley was being so disturbingly quiet.

The water finally shut off, and he came back inside, hair dripping, a towel wrapped around his waist.

"I made you a sandwich," I said lamely, pointing to it on the kitchen counter.

One side of his mouth quirked up, and he pulled me into a hug, getting the front of my dress all wet. I didn't care. A massive amount of tension left my body at his touch, and I frowned into his chest. He was hurting, and I'd been on edge because of it.

Fuck. I was catching feelings for the brother of the guy who could very well be the reason my brother was missing.

"Sorry for getting all moody," he said. "Seeing my brother just . . . It brings up some shit for me." He released me and dragged a hand down his face.

"Want to talk about it?"

He looked at me for a moment, opened his mouth, then gave me a sad little smile. "That's OK."

My heart fell. He wanted to; I could tell. But I'd been so adamant about not getting into personal shit.

I watched him eat the sandwich standing up, his back turned to me, while indecision churned in my gut. When he finished, he walked the plate over to the sink and leaned on it.

"I think I'm gonna go for a—"

"My brother is missing," I blurted, interrupting him.

*What the fuck?* I propped my hands on my hips and frowned at the ground. I'd wanted to share something with him, something personal, but not *that*.

He turned to face me, surprise written all over his face. "Do you . . ."

Whatever he saw in my eyes—fear, uncertainty, the sudden urge to run away—made him trail off.

A clap of thunder outside startled us both, and I realized it was raining. The electricity cut out, leaving so many unsaid things in the stifling darkness between us.

Riley walked over to me, took my hand, and led me outside. It was raining hard, water sluicing off the overhanging roof. It looked as if pizza on the beach wasn't going to happen. Not that I was up for it.

We sat down on the top step, the rain splashing onto our feet and ankles.

"My mom left us when I was twelve," Riley began. "Seth was nine. Our father is . . . a piece of shit. My childhood wasn't exactly fun. Dad's family has owned property inland for generations, but I don't know if every generation was so entitled, cruel, and immoral as my dad's. My family is into some illegal shit. I'm not going to go into details."

He squeezed my hand, and I scooted closer to him, our shoulders and legs pressed together.

"I still don't know what happened to my mom. Maybe she just cracked and couldn't take any more. Maybe she died, or someone . . ." *killed her*. I could hear the unspeakable thought at the edge of his lips. It made a shiver go down my spine.

What had I gotten myself into? What had Ben gotten himself into?

"Either way, Seth and I were left in the sole care of our father—and the dregs of society that always hang around him. He raised us in his image. I knew how to hotwire a car by the age of thirteen, was shooting cans at the back of the property before my fifteenth birthday, dropped out of school as soon as it wouldn't have CPS knocking on our door. You get the idea. Dad set the only example we had, and Seth and I followed it. A few years back . . ."

He took a deep breath and ran his hand through his hair. I'd never seen Riley nervous. I squeezed his hand, a silent encouragement to keep going, let his dirty past out, let the summer rain wash it away.

"A few years back," he started again, speaking louder over the intensifying rain. "I did some fucked-up shit. And I got caught. I kept my mouth shut about the others involved, and the judge decided to make an example of me. I went to prison. I was nineteen and sentenced to ten years. It scared the absolute shit out of me, but it got me away from my dad too, from this place. I got out after five—good behavior and overcrowding, I guess." He shrugged.

"Riley . . ." I caressed his arm, leaning more into him. The fact that he'd come out of prison a better man than he'd gone in was nothing short of remarkable.

"Don't." He shook his head. "Don't use that voice, full

of pity and heartbreak. I made mistakes, and I paid for them. I made my time count for something, got my GED, grew up. I got out two years ago. I planned to just move somewhere far away from here and start fresh, but parole required me to be in this state, and I really didn't have anywhere to go. I nearly went down that track again, being around my dad and his . . . people. But then I met Ziggy, and I got a job at Pelly's, and Pelly let me move into this place if I was willing to fix it up. It was practically falling apart."

He looked up and laughed. "I have plans, you know. There's nothing wrong with an honest paycheck bartending, but I want to see more of the world, do more with my life."

"Why haven't you?" I asked. He clearly had his shit together now.

"My brother." He sighed. "I want to get him out, show him that life doesn't have to be so ruthless, but . . . my dad's influence on him is strong."

He'd do anything for his brother, just as I would for mine. We had that much in common.

We had a lot *more* than that in common, but I wasn't willing to admit that just yet.

The longer I stayed here, the deeper I dug, the more complicated everything got.

I had to find Ben—no one else would—and I knew in my bones that something wasn't right. But my heart bled for Riley and his brother.

Riley asked if I wanted to talk about my brother, but I avoided the conversation, saying I wasn't ready. Instead we just sat on the porch, watching the rain, letting our legs get drenched. The summer rain wasn't cold, but it was coming down hard.

When the wind picked up and started sending the rain down at an angle, hitting as high as our faces, we still didn't move.

It was as if we'd made an unspoken agreement to sit there and ride out the storm together.

# CHAPTER EIGHT

Almost a week later, I sat in that same spot, watching the sunrise.

I'd been doing that a lot more lately—sitting on the steps and looking out at the water, the sunrise, the sunset, the rain, the moon and stars. I was struggling to sleep.

I'd been keeping as close an eye on Seth as possible, trying to catch his conversations when he came into Pelly's, encouraging Riley to talk about his past and his brother. I'd even asked Jess a few vague questions in the hope that she'd go into detail, but I didn't get anything of much use from her. She and Seth were the same age and had been friends since elementary school. She stayed away from his "business," but she clearly had a sisterly kind of love for both Seth and Riley.

I didn't feel as though I could tell her my whole story; I couldn't be sure she would support me. I wanted so badly to tell Riley, but that was more of a clusterfuck every day.

He was so patient and gentle, occasionally offering me opportunities to talk about my brother but giving me plenty of space when I didn't want to. He could tell something was off, though. I'd caught him staring at me over a meal, a pensive look on his face, several times. The night before last, he'd come out onto the porch with me at two in the morning when I'd gotten out of bed, unable to sleep. He'd just sat next to me, let me lean my head on his shoulder, and looked at the night sky with me.

Mostly, I wanted to corner Seth and demand answers. He had to know something about where Ben was. The hints at how dangerous his family was, the criminal connotations, it was all too much of a coincidence.

It was also why I couldn't just come out and ask him. I wasn't too proud to admit to myself that I was scared. He was a scary dude. I was in a town where I didn't really know anyone. No one even knew I was here—I'd made sure of it. What if I ended up like my brother? Just . . . gone.

But the constant lack of answers and the tension between Riley and me was getting to me. I'd need to make a move soon.

The gorgeous, complicated man himself came out onto the porch. He was still in his underwear and nothing else, carrying two steaming mugs of coffee.

"Three sugars and a splash of cream." He held one out for me. He knew how I took my coffee. I knew how he took his too. And that he didn't like pickles. And exactly how quickly I could make him come with my mouth.

"Thank you." I gave him a genuine smile as I took the coffee.

"How long have you been up?" he asked, sitting next to me.

"I wanted to watch the sunrise," I lied, and something in my chest tightened. I'd grown to hate lying to him. It didn't feel right.

He didn't call me out on it, just took a sip of his coffee

and started telling me about his late shift the night before. He'd gotten to bed after three, and here he was, barely an hour after sunrise, making me coffee.

His chattering soothed my frayed nerves as the coffee warmed my soul.

Riley went from talking about the incompetent new bar chick he'd had to train the night before, to telling me about some old friends from high school that had come into Pelly's, to recalling some of his childhood memories.

"We used to get up to so much shit." He laughed. "Like, normal preteen shit, not the hardcore criminal shit I was doing at home. How fucked up is that? Anyway, I remember this one time, it must've been early summer or something, because it was a Tuesday but we weren't at school, and we got the bright idea to improve hang eight. I think the whole town hated that thing, and we were being smartasses, so we got a bunch of stuff to make paper-mache. We were going to add a tentacle to the surfer dude, then put—"

"What did you just say?" I turned to look at him, my coffee and the shimmering water forgotten.

"Hmm?" he hummed around a sip of his own coffee. "About me and my friends running amok around town? What? Teenagers don't do stupid shit where you're from?" He chuckled.

"No, you mentioned hengeit or something. What is that?"

"Oh, yeah. That's the statue of the surfer and octopus in the park." He gestured over his shoulder with his thumb. "All the locals call it that because hang ten . . . and the octopus, so . . . *hang eight* . . . You all right?" He frowned at me.

I was *not* all right. Or maybe I was more all right than

I'd been in a long time. I wasn't sure, but my face must've looked as if I'd seen a ghost.

"Holy shit," I breathed. The one clue my brother had given me had been there this whole time. It was visible from the beach. I'd walked past it countless times. I'd even drawn it in my notebook.

I'd spent two weeks relaxing, getting lost in Riley and his stories and his embrace, forgetting why I was really here. I was such an idiot. My brother was missing, and here I was enjoying a morning coffee.

I'd wasted so much time, but I wasn't about to waste any more.

Riley was saying something, probably worried I'd had a mental break of some kind, but I hardly heard him. I tipped the rest of my coffee out on the sand aggressively. I wished I could spill my guilt out along with it, and my stupidity, let all the dark contents of my heart mingle with the aromatic brew and soak into the soft grains.

I left the cup on the step, got to my feet, and took off up the beach.

"Chloe!" Riley called after me. "Where are you going? Fuck."

The sound of the screen door slamming registered behind me, but I didn't care if he'd stormed inside, pissed at me, or if he was rushing to put pants on to follow me.

I broke into a jog, desperate not to waste another second.

The beach was nearly empty. Only an older couple walking their dog and a few early surfers out on the water. Everything was silent, the town only just waking up on a lazy Sunday morning.

It felt almost surreal to tear through that sleepy serenity with my hurried steps and manic energy.

I was panting by the time I made it all the way to the other side of the beach. Running on sand was hard work. But I didn't stop when I reached the paved pathway. One part trailed off toward the water, in the direction of the pier. The other one wound through the park, right past the statue.

While the beach had a few people around, the park was completely deserted. I had no one but birds to keep me company as I descended on the statue like a madwoman.

*I'm stashing it at* hang eight *under the tunas.* What the hell did that mean? There was a surfboard, a surfer, an octopus, but no tuna in sight.

. . . *at hang eight* under *the tunas.* He'd sounded rushed in the voicemail, scared even. The most logical explanation was that he was being literal—or as literal as he could be.

Lungs still burning, I picked my way through the flowers and rosebushes surrounding the ridiculous statue and walked around it. I inspected it closely, looking for any cracks or indents, anything that looked as if you could hide an object in there. I was on my third rotation, focusing on the base where it met the garden bed, when Riley showed up.

Apparently he'd run inside to put pants on.

"Chloe. What the hell? What are you doing?" He sounded winded too. I glanced at him briefly but didn't reply. Looked as if he'd *only* put pants on. He wasn't even wearing shoes or a shirt. Sweat glistened on his chest. The morning heat was already oppressive—it was going to be a stinking-hot day.

Frustrated with not seeing anything that looked like a clue, I dropped to my knees and started digging at the moist dirt with my bare hands. *Under*—he'd said it would be under the tunas. There was no other option as far as I could see. Whatever he wanted me to find had to be buried.

But how deep? And where exactly? It would take me all day to thoroughly check every inch of the soil around the base of the statue, and whatever it was may not even be there. I didn't care if it took two damn days. I wasn't going to eat or sleep until I found whatever it was. Or until I collapsed.

Riley appeared in front of me and dropped to his knees, blocking my methodical path through the dirt. I gave him an annoyed look.

"Chloe," he said, his voice gentle, wary. "Stop. Tell me what's going on."

His eyes were pleading and wide. He must've been so confused, probably frightened that he'd shacked up with a crazy bitch. But I just didn't have the time or space to consider anyone else's sensibilities. I knew I was being obsessive. I didn't care.

"*You* stop," I said, slapping at his knees so I could keep digging under them. "I have to find the . . . the thing."

"What thing? What are you looking for?" he asked, shuffling out of my way. I didn't answer, and after a few moments, he'd had enough of my bullshit.

"Chloe!" He gripped my upper arms and forced me to look at him. "Talk to me."

He didn't look pissed. He genuinely looked as if he wanted to help, to comfort me.

Something inside me cracked—a deep fissure right through my chest—and to my horror, tears started falling down my cheeks.

He pulled me in for a hug and held me tightly, gently rocking us from side to side. He didn't let go, telling me with his actions that he was here for me.

But would he be when he found out the whole truth? Could I risk telling him all of it? I wanted to so badly.

I pulled back, and he let me go and sat back on his heels. I mirrored his position and wiped at my tears. I was going to tell him as much as I could. As much as I felt was safe.

"I'm here for my brother. About seven weeks ago, I got a weird-ass voicemail from Ben in the middle of the night. He mentioned hiding something at hang eight. I had no idea what he was talking about, but then he just stopped calling or taking calls. I knew he was here in Verbena Cove the last time we spoke, so I came here to find him. Then you mentioned the statue, and it clicked. Whatever he wanted me to find has to be around here somewhere."

I shrugged, partly indicating I didn't know what else to say, partly saying this was why I was acting like a deranged person.

Riley just watched me for a few beats, then asked: "Do you know what he hid? What you're looking for?"

It wasn't the question I'd been expecting. I'd braced myself for questions about why I didn't call the police and why I hadn't said anything before and all the other shit I was hoping to avoid telling him. I wanted to deflect and make him leave so I could get back to work, but he'd taken me by surprise by asking something practical.

"No." I shook my head. "No idea."

"OK." Riley got to his feet and stepped over the flowers and bushes, walking around the statue and disappearing.

I hadn't been expecting that either. But I guess he'd done what I wanted him to—he'd left me alone so I could get back to clawing at the dirt with my bare hands.

So why did it feel . . . wrong? I felt hurt at his abrupt departure.

Before I could start crying like a little baby again, I forced myself to focus and got back to work.

Barely a few minutes had passed before Riley interrupted me again. He appeared next to me and dropped a shovel onto the mess I'd created.

"Borrowed some tools from a buddy nearby." He gave me a small smile. "I'll start on the other side. It'll be quicker."

Without waiting for a response, he tightened his grip on another shovel and walked around the statue. A moment later, I could hear the distinct, rhythmic sound of a shovel hitting dirt.

For the second time that morning, my eyes stung from tears because of this man. Not only was he rolling with my crazy; he was actively participating. To have someone's support like that was . . . almost indescribable for me.

I swallowed the tears back and picked up the shovel. We fell into a rhythm, digging up the top foot or so of soil and sifting through it with our hands for anything that shouldn't be there. At least an hour had passed when we met in the middle, a perfect circle of mess around the statue.

We were both breathing hard and sweating. The temperature was rising with the sun, and the town was waking up. More cars were driving past on the road nearby, and two joggers had run past, giving us weird looks.

"We should get some water," Riley said, sitting down and wiping his brow with the back of his hand.

I plonked my butt down in the dirt next to him, looking at how big the surrounding flower bed was. Even with two of us and shovels, this was going to take all day.

"Fuck," I breathed, looking at all the pretty flowers and feeling a little defeated.

"Yeah." Riley nodded. "We're gonna be here awhile.

Until someone realizes we're destroying public property and Sheriff Gibson has to get his butt out of his air-conditioned office to come down here and arrest us for vandalism."

"I think we can outrun him." I hadn't met the sheriff, but from what Riley had told me, it sounded as though he'd gotten soft in his easy job policing a quiet beachside town.

Riley snorted, then groaned as he pushed to his feet. "I'll go get us some water and food."

He gingerly stepped over the gardenias, forget-me-nots, and gladiolas. I wasn't sure why he bothered. We were about to systematically rip them from the ground anyway.

I stared at the pretty blooms, planted in a neat pattern, and felt bad for what we were about to do.

Riley had started to walk across the grass when I registered another bloom in the corners of the flower bed. A memory hit me so hard I almost fell over.

"Riley!" I scrambled to my feet and carefully shuffled past the plants myself, now that I hoped we wouldn't have to murder them all.

He turned around and rushed back to me. "What is it?"

I pointed at the unassuming flowers. "Petunias, right?"

"Yeah?"

"My grandma used to have them all throughout her garden. She loved them. They lined her entire driveway. Ben used to call them *tunas* when he was little. Couldn't get the pronunciation right."

We looked at each other, then back down to the little plant.

"You start on this one. I'll get the next one over," he said, going to grab the shovels.

We got to work, and within ten minutes, we'd dug up two of the corner plants. I dropped to my knees and felt around in the dirt, even poked around the roots still attached to the plant. Nothing.

I looked over to Riley and found him sitting back on his heels, watching me, a pile of dirt in front of him. He shook his head.

I sighed, and we both got up and moved to the last two plants.

A middle-aged couple on a leisurely walk slowed down to frown in confusion at us. The frowns turned to suspicion and disapproval as they walked away. They glanced back several times, whispering to each other. A cyclist went by, then another.

We were running out of time. Before long someone would either confront us or call the cops.

I stuck the shovel into the dirt right near the base of the plant. I couldn't be too aggressive with the digging, and it was slowing us down. I had no idea what I was looking for and didn't want to risk damaging it.

I shifted some dirt from around the plant, then wedged the shovel under it and started to push the petunias up out of the ground. Something glinted in the sun, catching my eye.

"Riley!" I called frantically, dropping to my knees.

He stopped what he was doing and sprinted to my side.

"I saw something. Can you just hold the . . ."

He pulled the plant to the side, tugging the roots out of the way so I could claw at the spot that I'd seen glint. I dug around, and then my fingers brushed against something smooth.

I shifted dirt out of the way and wrapped my fingers around what was clearly a phone. When I pulled it out, Riley let the plant settle back into its spot.

I brushed the soil off the device, revealing my brother's Pickle Rick case.

"It's my brother's phone." I looked up at Riley with wide eyes. Part of me couldn't quite believe we'd actually found something.

I tried turning it on, but of course it was dead. It had been in the ground for weeks. Maybe it wasn't even functional anymore.

"Go plug it in." Riley gestured to the beach and his shack on the other side of it. "I'll fix this mess."

"Are you sure?" I looked at all the soil and the dug-up plants, wincing. I'd feel guilty just leaving him there, especially since the area was getting busier. I didn't want him to get in trouble because of me.

"Chloe, go," he said firmly as we got to our feet. I wrapped my filthy arms around his neck and kissed him, putting all my gratitude and appreciation into the kiss.

"Thank you, Riley," I said fervently against his mouth.

The full truth of the situation and his brother's potential involvement was surely going to come out soon, but I hoped it wouldn't get between us.

I knew as I turned and rushed back to the shack that I was being naive. He'd feel betrayed. I'd worry about him trying to protect his brother. He'd certainly throw me out.

For the third time that morning, tears pushed at the backs of my eyes because of Riley.

This time, as I thought about losing him, I couldn't stop them from creating tracks down my dirty cheeks.

# CHAPTER NINE

The trek back to the shack was slower. I'd spent all my energy sprinting to the statue and then digging, so the best I could manage was a brisk walk. I got a lot of weird looks from the people enjoying the hot summer beach day.

I couldn't blame them. I would've gawked at the disheveled, panting, covered-in-literal-dirt crazy chick too.

Ben had the same model mobile phone as me, so I beelined for my charger in the corner of the kitchenette. Dusting the phone off as best I could with a tea towel, I plugged it in and leaned on the counter, waiting to see if it would work.

After a few moments, the battery symbol popped up on the screen. I released a massive breath and leaned on the counter. It lived.

Now that I'd achieved what I'd single-mindedly set out to do that morning, all the energy was draining out of my system. The adrenaline and sheer determination were evaporating, leaving my limbs feeling wobbly and my head woozy. I shuffled toward the couch, ready to collapse, but halfway across the room, I remembered how filthy I was and changed direction.

I went through the bathroom and headed for the outdoor shower. After swinging the privacy screen closed, I turned the water on, peeled my clothes off, and left them in a gross brown pile on the ground.

I fully intended to wash myself like a responsible adult, but I just didn't have any energy left. Instead, I lowered myself to the ground and let the cool water pelt my back while I leaned my head on my knees.

I have no idea how long I sat there, letting the water turn the dirt to mud and swirl down the drain. Riley opened the screen, startling me and making me whip my head up to look at him.

How long *had* I been sitting there? Putting the flower bed to rights would've taken some time.

"Hey, you." He smiled, leaning on the wall next to the showerhead.

"Hey." I wiped the droplets off my face and slowly got to my feet. He helped me up with a firm grip on my arms.

"How much water have you wasted?" he asked, but I could hear the amusement in his voice.

"No idea. How long ago did I leave?"

"About half an hour." He pushed his shorts down and dumped them on top of my pile. "A couple of buddies came past, and I roped them into helping."

I watched as he stepped under the stream, face turned up to the water, dirt washing away. He scrubbed himself quickly, then turned the water off. Apparently I really had been wasting it. I'd left it on for over half an hour, and I wasn't really sure what his hot-water situation was.

Why the hell was I thinking about Riley's hot-water setup?

"Hey," he whispered, stroking my cheek to get my attention.

I looked at him and fought off tears. One way or another, everything was about to change. Once we stepped out of this shower, I'd check what was on Ben's phone. Riley would learn the whole truth. I'd have answers I had a feeling I didn't want to know.

I wasn't ready to face it—face losing him.

I guess he wasn't either. He wrapped his hand around the back of my neck and pulled me in for a kiss. I returned it enthusiastically, my hands wrapping around his waist and pulling him closer.

His hands roamed my body, gripping and caressing as though he wasn't sure which part of me he wanted to hold on to the most. I could feel him harden between us, his arousal and desperation only driving my own higher.

I bit his bottom lip, and he hissed. Picking me up with a firm grip under my thighs, he spun me around and slammed me against the wall. The showerhead dripped onto my tits, and he leaned down to lick at the droplets before sucking on my nipples.

I moaned and reached between us.

Riley met my gaze as he pushed into me. We fucked just like that—staring into each other's souls, frantic, desperate, never looking away.

My orgasm was bittersweet, regret riding the ecstasy. The peak was the end, and I wasn't ready.

He followed me mere seconds after, finally breaking eye contact to turn his face up to the sky and groan.

After he set me on my feet, we held each other close for several long moments, his cum dripping down my thigh. I couldn't even think about the implications of the fact we'd just had unprotected sex. My brain could only deal with so much at a time.

I couldn't put it off any longer.

With a sigh, I reached for the tap and turned the shower back on. We rinsed off once more, then dried off and pulled on some clothes. We didn't speak the entire time.

With a nervous breath, I marched over to Ben's phone and stared at it. Riley stepped up next to me and took my hand. I couldn't help but admire his quiet patience, his steady calm.

He must've had a million questions. He was a smart guy. He must've started to put at least some things together after this morning. Yet, there he stood, at my side, lending me his strength.

I pressed the power button and waited.

As soon as the phone turned on, dozens of notifications started coming through. Missed calls, messages, social media—all of Ben's online life pouring in at once. I waited a few moments for it to stop vibrating, then picked it up. It unlocked without asking for a passcode. He *always* had a passcode on his phone. He must've removed it before burying the thing.

Where to start? I navigated to his call log. Plenty of missed calls from me, some from Mom and Dad, his friends from back home, numbers and names I didn't recognize. This wasn't telling me anything.

I went to messages next. Again, a lot from me, and a lot from names I didn't know. I was too impatient to go methodically through each one. I went to his camera roll, and a familiar photo caught my attention.

Acutely aware of Riley by my side, his hand still clutching mine, I opened the picture of our brothers together with Verbena Cove beach shining bright behind them.

Riley became very still.

With a thick swallow I looked up at him. He met my gaze, but I didn't find accusation there, or anger. Just a bit of confusion.

He was starting to put the picture together, but he didn't have all the pieces of the puzzle yet. We were in the same boat there.

I scrolled through Ben's photos slowly. A few more pics of him and Seth and a few other guys. Some shots from a party. A selfie with a chick who was all over him. Some scenic shots around Verbena Cove.

The most recent thing in the camera roll was a video. I pressed play.

It was dark, hard to make out what the camera was pointing at. Voices could be heard in the distance, but I couldn't decipher what they were saying. I turned the volume up to max, but they'd stopped speaking.

The camera slowly panned to the side, around whatever was blocking the view. A shed or barn type of building came into the shot. It was clearly nighttime, but several lights hanging from the high ceiling illuminated sections of the space, casting the corners in shadow.

"What the fu . . ." Riley breathed, leaning in closer. "That's my dad's property. That's—"

He cut himself off as his brother turned to face the camera, and the shot went dark again for a few moments. More voices saying things we couldn't make out, then Ben inched the camera back into view again.

Several men stood around with Seth, and one was sitting in a chair. Ben zoomed in a bit. Not sitting—*tied* to a chair.

Seth leaned down, said something into the man's ear, then straightened to his full height and shot him in the head.

I jumped. The phone fell out of my grasp and clattered to the counter as I took a step back, my hands covering my mouth.

I couldn't look at Riley, but I could hear him breathing hard, could feel the tension in every part of his body—it matched mine.

He picked the phone back up and rewound to just after his brother blew someone's brains out. I leaned in, gritting my teeth against the overwhelming wave of emotion threatening to drown me.

In the video, Ben gasped and moved the camera until only a faint outline of a dark door was visible.

"Who's there?" someone called, the rough voice echoing in the cavernous space.

The picture blurred, and we could hear shuffling and then running.

The video ended.

This was so much worse than anything I'd ever imagined. So, so much worse.

# CHAPTER TEN

I told Riley everything. I felt as if I was losing my mind, as if I was trying to process too much information at once and I just couldn't do it.

So I stood in Riley's kitchen, tears falling down my cheeks, and I told him. About how I grew up, my parents, Ben, how he stopped calling. I even played the voicemail to him on my phone. I told him about how I came to Verbena Cove to look for my brother, how that girl warned me off looking for him, how I got nowhere for weeks and ran out of money.

When I was done, I felt drained. Riley wasn't saying anything—just leaning on the counter and staring at the floor with a deep frown. I took a shaky, cleansing breath and grabbed a kitchen towel to wipe the tears and snot off my face.

"So, you didn't shack up with me to get closer to my brother?" he asked, his voice flat.

"*What?*" I stepped closer to him, aching to touch him, but I stopped myself at the last second. "Riley. No. I had no idea who Seth even was. I only realized he was your brother when he showed up at Pelly's that day. You saw me that night on the beach. Do you really think I would've deliberately starved myself on the off chance that you'd find me? Come *on*."

He looked up at me, and I realized he wasn't pissed or suspicious. His gaze was full of vulnerability, uncertainty. He was teetering on the edge of hurt.

He reached out for me, and I fell against him with relief.

I couldn't lose him.

But could I trust him? Now that he knew the full story, would he try to stop me from finding Ben? He was pretty hell-bent on helping his brother.

I hated that I was having these thoughts, but I was reeling, my brain trying desperately to catch up. One thing I knew for sure—it felt insanely good to be held by Riley, to feel his arms steadying me.

I closed my eyes and just took a moment to feel some comfort, some relief that I'd told the full story to someone and didn't need to carry it all on my own.

Then I snapped my eyes open again. "Oh, god, I wasted so much time."

Riley pulled back only enough to look at me properly, questions in his gaze.

"I should've gone to the . . ." I trailed off. I'd gone to the police back home, and they hadn't been able to do anything. Until a few moments ago, I didn't have Ben's phone or that video or anything else to take to them. That was the whole reason I'd come here. To find answers.

It still felt as though I'd wasted time. But I wasn't willing to waste a *second* more now that I did have something to take to them.

"I have to go. I have to show the police the video." I

pulled Ben's phone off the charger and turned to look for my shoes, but Riley grabbed my arm.

"Chloe, wait." He tugged me back to his side. "You can't do that."

I raised my eyebrows slowly. "My brother is missing. You saw what was on that video."

"Yes." He dropped my arm. "And if you take it to the police station here in town, you're not going to get very far with any of this. Three guys work there. I know them all. The two deputies don't have two brain cells to rub together, and the sheriff is in my father's pocket. That phone will disappear as soon as you hand it over. They're not going to do jack shit."

"Then I'll go somewhere else." The nearest city was a good two-hour drive away, and I had no way to get there, but I also had no reason to hide where I was from my parents anymore. I'd just use the credit card. "Jess has a car. I'll pay her to drive me."

I found my flip-flops, stepped into them, and headed for the bedroom to grab the card out of my bag. With it tucked in my back pocket, I made for the door, but Riley stepped in front of me.

"You're not thinking clearly, Chloe." He was blocking my way with his body, and I once again questioned my decision to tell him everything and let him watch the video with me.

"Fuck you," I said, my voice steady, as I lifted my chin in defiance. "My brother is missing. For the first time, I actually have something that I can do about it. Get out of my way, Riley."

"Just listen to me." He moved out of the way but was begging me with his eyes to hear him out.

I huffed and crossed my arms over my chest. He took it

as permission to keep speaking.

"I'm not saying don't go to the cops, OK? I'm not trying to get you to drop this. But I know my brother. I know my family. It's not going to be as simple as handing the video over to the cops. Just let me do some digging first."

"What? Why?" I was losing patience.

"Let me go to my father's property, see what they have going on up there, see who's around. See if I can find out if they're keeping your brother in one of the buildings there. I'll try to take some pictures too. We'll make copies of everything, and we'll take it to multiple police precincts. The more evidence we have, the less chance there is of this not getting resolved."

"Why would you do that? Stick your neck out for me? Against your family, no less." I frowned. What if he went there and warned them? What if they all disappeared? What if he brought them back here and *I* disappeared?

"Because I lo—" He cut himself off, fear in his eyes. Then he squared his shoulders, and a determined look replaced the fear. "Because I love you, Chloe. Because I know what my family is doing is wrong, and I'm not willing to lose you because of it."

Well, shit. I was not expecting that.

He took my hands in his. "I'm asking you to trust me. Please, Chloe. Let me go there and see what I can find out."

Maybe I'd live to regret it, but deep down inside, I'd decided to let him try the moment he said those three monumental words to me.

"Go," I whispered.

He kissed me on the forehead and rushed out the door, leaving me standing in his home alone, the sound of the endless ocean my only company.

———

I stood at the edge of the water, the waves kissing my feet as I tried to match my breathing to their rhythm.

Riley had been gone for over two hours, and the sun was beginning to set. For the first time since arriving in Verbena Cove, I didn't feel calmed by watching the colors in the sky change.

I'd gone through Ben's phone almost obsessively. I read all his messages, going back at least a few months; went through the photos more carefully; checked all his social media; googled some of the numbers that had called him. None of it was useful in any way. The only thing on that phone that was related to where he might be was that awful video.

I couldn't bring myself to watch it again. I felt sick every time I even thought about it.

After sending myself a copy of the video and saving it to my drive, as well as forwarding it to two other email addresses, I packed my bag. I'd picked it up several times, ready to walk out and just go to the police, Riley be damned.

But every time I marched out onto that porch, I found myself looking for him, hoping he'd walk around those rocks by the water and tell me everything would be OK.

In the end, I'd decided to just watch one last sunset. If he wasn't back by the time night set in, I was leaving.

Footsteps in the sand behind me made me turn, and there he was, walking toward me from the house. He must've come in through the front door.

The relief at seeing his face was palpable. He hadn't left me.

I met him halfway, and we hugged, holding on to each other as if something was trying to tear us apart.

"So?" I asked, pulling back to look at him.

Riley released a heavy breath, something between frustration and worry in his expression. "Seth wasn't there."

"What?" I loosened my grip, but he held on tighter.

"Apparently, he left this morning to take care of some business. I hung around with some of the guys, had a few beers, listened in on some conversations. I didn't want to raise suspicion by asking questions—they know I want nothing to do with that life—but I picked up enough to know he'll be back in a few days. Dad wasn't there either, so I'm guessing they went together. And no sign of Ben, but I wasn't able to check all the outbuildings."

*How convenient.* I hated that I thought it, but what was I meant to think?

This time when I released my hold, he let me go.

"OK, so we go to the police with what we have." I nodded.

"Chloe . . ." He shook his head regretfully.

"You can't be serious!"

"They'll never find them. One of the guys here will tip them off, and they will just disappear. Then you'll never know what happened to Ben."

"Then we go back to your dad's property and search for him."

"That's a surefire way to get shot—if we can make it over the electric fence. And he may not even be there."

"I can't just sit on this, Riley. And just so you know, I've already made copies of the video and saved it in several locations. This is getting out one way or another."

He reeled back as if I'd slapped him. "You think I'd try to . . . I'm trying to help you here, Chloe."

He sounded as frustrated as I felt.

I stared him down. There was no point arguing. I wanted to just walk away. Take my bag and leave like I'd been trying to. Do what I knew was right.

But the sand was keeping me right where I was, my toes sinking into it farther and farther. This place, this beach, this man . . . it had an unnatural hold on me.

Riley's face fell, all the frustration draining from it.

"I'm sorry." He caressed my arms. "I know them. They will be back in a few days. They always are. I'm just trying to make sure they're around when the cops come to arrest them. That's all. If you want to go to the police now, we can."

I chewed my lip and looked out to the water. Night had fallen, and the water looked ominously black, full of unseen secrets and dangers—just like this town.

I wanted the best possible chance of finding my brother. Maybe that meant going to the police immediately. Maybe it meant waiting for Seth to come back. I had no idea.

All I knew was that I wasn't done with Verbena Cove, and that some confused part of me really did trust Riley.

# CHAPTER ELEVEN

A wave crashed against my chest, splashing me in the face and nearly taking my bikini top with it. The midday sun was beating down on my head. I could just hear the voices of hundreds of people on the main beach on the other side of the rocks, cooling off in the water just as I was.

When the next wave came roaring at me, I dove under it, letting the salty water drown out the rest of the world.

If only it could drown out my thoughts too.

It had been three days since I dug Ben's phone out of the ground with my bare hands and uncovered an unspeakable crime.

I'd been worried about him since the day I received his last voicemail, but now it was worse. Knowing what he'd seen, how dangerous the people he'd been hanging out with were—I was consumed by thoughts of where he might be, how badly he might be hurt, whether I'd ever see him again.

No longer able to hold my breath, I kicked off and came up for air. Then I let the waves push me back toward shore.

Sand stuck to my wet feet as I walked onto the beach and headed for the shade of the porch. I settled into one of the chairs to dry off but immediately felt the urge to go back in the water. Sitting still was becoming almost impossible. I constantly felt restless, had hardly slept the past few nights, and had dropped my tray of dirty dishes three times during the one shift I'd made myself go to.

Riley had suggested we go to the police a few times now. The first time was when he found me sitting on the porch in the dark in the middle of the night. He said all the right things, even did all the right things. He comforted me when he could tell I was struggling, constantly offered to talk about it, and yes, even offered to go to the police, saying he couldn't stand to see me like this anymore.

The few times he'd suggested it had resulted in arguments. The fact was, I just didn't know the right thing to do. I felt as though I was drowning with indecision, unable to trust my own instincts, frozen in fear of making the wrong move.

At night, we came together. We held each other and caressed each other and kissed deeply. We made love every night. It wasn't fucking anymore, not after what he'd said to me that day. I still couldn't bring myself to say it back, but my body was saying it every time.

During the day, though, things were tense.

Riley's sleepy voice came floating out the screen door, carrying through the house from the bedroom. I couldn't make out what he was saying, but clearly, he was up.

He'd worked the late shift, and I'd been careful not to wake him when I got up that morning. I didn't want to talk to him right now, though—it seemed easier to put off the tension just a little longer—so I stood up to get back in the water.

But before I could make it to the stairs, I heard his footsteps come thudding through the house, and the screen door burst open. He stopped in front of me, hair a mess and eyes wide, the impression of the pillow crease on his left cheek.

My heart started hammering. "What?"

"Seth's back in town."

"Are you sure?" I gripped his hands, holding on for dear life.

"Yeah. Just spoke with a buddy who bumped into him as we were on the phone."

"OK." I dropped his hands and shook mine out, suddenly feeling frazzled. This was what we'd been waiting for, right? So why did I feel as though I wasn't sure what the next move was?

I forced myself to take a deep breath. "Right. He's back. Let's get moving then. Let's go to the police."

I rushed into the house, pulled a T-shirt and shorts over my bikini, and searched for shoes. Why could I never find damn shoes in this place?

"Chloe, wait." Riley followed me in and pulled clothes on himself.

"Wait for what?" I frowned at him for a second, then grabbed Ben's phone and mine, dug my flip-flops out from under the couch, and headed back outside.

"Dammit, Chloe, *wait.*" Riley grabbed my elbow, forcing me to turn around. He looked as frazzled and worked up as I did. "Let me go talk to him."

I took a step away from him. This could not be happening. Was he *serious*?

He must've seen the outraged look on my face, because he rushed to explain. "I *know*, OK? I know Seth's done some unforgiveable shit, and I'm not suggesting he should get away with it. But he's still my brother. I just want to talk to him, see if I can convince him to turn himself in. It will be better for him if he does. He may have a chance of turning his life around like I did."

Riley had a serious savior complex. How had I not seen it before? Jess had mentioned that he helped her get her shit together last year. He'd taken me in, knowing literally nothing about me. And his brother . . . his brother was probably the reason for his need to save other people the same way he'd saved himself. He hadn't been able to get through to Seth, so he was filling that need with others.

Now time had run out, and Riley was still desperately grasping at the idea that he could save his little brother from the life Seth had clearly already embraced.

At the expense of *my* brother.

"God, I'm such an idiot." I shook my head. "I believed you. I actually trusted you when you said it would be better to wait until he got back. But you were just buying time. You were stalling so you could . . ." Emotion was choking me, making it hard to get the words out.

"No." He shook his head. He looked desperate, torn. "That's not it at all. I'm not asking you *not* to go to the police. I'm just asking you to let me get Seth to go to them first."

"You're asking me to risk him laughing in your face and disappearing because you're going to warn him!" I was yelling. It was the only way to force the words out.

"I won't let that happen!" Riley yelled too. Not in anger, not at me, just raising his voice so he could be heard.

As if they were answering our shouting, someone screamed in the distance.

Riley and I both snapped our heads in the direction of the main beach.

That was not the kind of scream we heard all the time— the kind that came from that first splash of cold water or the excitement of kids unable to hold it in as they chased each other.

This was not a carefree scream.

It was a guttural scream of pure fear.

It came again, another joining it, followed by the sound of several people shouting things we couldn't make out.

Whatever was going on out there, I didn't want to know. I had to focus on my own clusterfuck. But I had to go past the main beach to get to town and find Jess anyway, so it was a good excuse to rush away from Riley.

He stayed on my heels, though, probably excited at the prospect of someone else to save. We waded through ankle-deep water, between the big rocks, and then rushed onto the main beach. A crowd was gathering about a hundred feet away, near the water's edge.

I should've walked away. I should've marched right up the beach and through the parking area.

But I didn't. I went on a diagonal, keeping an eye on the commotion out of the corner of my eye.

As I got closer, a few people shifted, and I caught a glimpse of what they were all staring at.

I stopped abruptly, and then everything washed over me like the waves did. Only this time, I couldn't kick up to the surface for air.

# CHAPTER TWELVE

nother scream tore through the tranquility of the beach, only this time it was me screaming. The sound that came out of my throat was pure anguish.

A body had washed up on the beach. It looked bloated and half-eaten by whatever sea creatures had got to it.

It was my brother.

His favorite Air Jordans were still on his feet; the platinum bracelet I'd gotten him for his twenty-first birthday glinted in the sun.

Ben was dead.

My sweet, caring, passionate, headstrong brother was dead.

The only person in this world who had ever understood me was dead.

I shoved people out of the way unceremoniously until I was right by his side. I dropped to my knees in the wet sand, tears blurring my view of the horrific state he was in.

"No, no, no, no, no," I wailed, rocking back and forth.

Riley appeared next to me, and his arm wrapped around my shoulders.

"Don't touch me!" I screamed, shoving him off.

The people gathered around the scene were watching me, some with pity in their eyes, some with nothing more than morbid curiosity. I wanted to scream at them all, tell them to get away from us, to stop looking. They didn't deserve to see him like this. Ben didn't deserve this.

I sobbed and folded forward, my shaky fingers reaching out to touch the bracelet. It was cool against my skin.

Riley was still there, not touching me but hovering close.

"Chloe," he said in a low voice. "Don't look."

I threw him an angry glare. Who was he to tell me what to do when my brother was lying in the sand *dead*?

His gaze was soft, patient. "You don't want to remember him like this."

I started sobbing again. I had no control over my emotions or my body.

Riley was still here, still by my side, still trying to save me. I gave in and leaned against him. As soon as he took some of my weight, all my strength left me, and I clutched at him desperately, my whole body shaking.

He didn't say anything else. Just picked me up, said something to the police who had shown up, and walked away.

I couldn't stop crying.

All I could see was Ben's body in the sand.

All I could feel was Riley's touch.

Next thing I knew, he was lowering me to the couch in his living area.

I cried as I'd never cried in my life before. It was ugly and raw and made me choke on the air that Ben would never breathe again.

Riley held me through it all. Passing me tissues, stroking my back, whispering words I couldn't process.

Minutes or hours later, my tears dried up. I felt like a husk of myself—completely empty of emotions or thoughts.

Riley gently maneuvered me so I was lying down, and I let him. I wanted it all to go away. I wanted oblivion so badly that my body obliged, and I fell into a deep, dreamless sleep.

———

I awoke to the smell of grilled cheese and mint tea.

"How long was I out?" My voice was croaky from all the crying and screaming. My head throbbed as I sat up.

"A couple of hours," Riley replied, bringing over a plate with cheesy goodness on it and a steaming mug of tea.

I looked out the back window. It was late afternoon, the sky glowing golden.

I didn't understand how the day could dare to be so beautiful when my brother was dead.

Tears stung my eyes, my throat tightening. I didn't know how my body even had any liquid left after how much I'd cried earlier.

"You haven't eaten all day, baby." Riley sat next to me and held the plate out.

It reminded me so much of that first night we met. He'd forced his burger and his help on me when I needed it most.

Now he was forcing his kindness on me even though his brother had . . .

*Oh god.* I couldn't even think it.

"I'm not hungry."

"I know. Eat it anyway," he insisted. "You don't do well on an empty stomach, as we both well know."

I gave him a flat look. "Who cares? Nothing matters anymore."

I'd failed him. Ben had probably already been dead by the time I got my ass to Verbena Cove.

"*You matter*," Riley said with so much conviction that I was momentarily taken aback. "You're going to need your strength for what comes next, so just eat."

I picked up the damn sandwich and forced down every bite as we sat in silence, watching the room slowly getting darker.

"What comes next?" I asked, lifting the tea to my lips but gagging when I tried to sip it. I hated mint tea. I returned the mug to the table and chugged a glass of water instead.

"You'll have to talk to the police. Tell them everything. Show them the video. You'll need to call your parents too."

I groaned and dropped my head into my hands.

I'd been wanting to go to the police so badly for the past few days. Now all I wanted to do was lie back down and pretend this wasn't happening.

"Riley!" Seth called from out on the beach, his voice still a distance away but clearly heading here. And just like that, electricity surged through my limbs, and I saw red.

"I'm gonna fucking kill him," I growled, shooting to my feet and heading for the door.

I didn't even make it three steps. Riley grabbed me around the waist and pulled me back against him. I took a big lungful of air, ready to breathe fire at both of them, but he clamped his big hand over my mouth.

"Think for a second, Chloe," he said in a rush, close to my ear.

"Riley!" Seth called again, much closer.

I was going to gouge his eyes out with my nails. Scream my sorrow at him until his ears bled.

"He's twice your size, and I guarantee he's armed." Riley was talking fast now. Seth's footsteps could be heard in the sand, approaching fast. "It may not have been him."

I screamed into his hand and thrashed against him. That fucking asshole. His brother had killed mine, and he expected me to just let him go out there and help the cunt run from the police.

"It could've been him," Riley went on. "It could've. But it could've been my dad too. Or any one of the guys in that video. Don't you want justice for Ben? Don't you want to make sure that the right person pays for your brother's death?"

I sagged against him. I was crying again, my tears falling over Riley's fingers.

"Bro!" Seth pounded on the closed porch door. Why was the porch door closed? It was never closed.

It was dark in the house and getting darker and darker outside. He wouldn't be able to see us through the window.

"I'll make sure he doesn't go anywhere, OK? I'll get as much info out of him as I can. You take Ben's phone and go straight to the police. There are feds at the station already. Even Sheriff Gibson can't sweep a dead body under the sand. Show them the video and send them to Ziggy's. I'll take him there."

"Riley!" Seth sounded frantic.

"Coming!" Riley called.

Then he slowly removed his hand from my mouth, his hold on my waist loosening until it was more like a lover's embrace and less like the grip of a kidnapper.

"I love you." He kissed my temple and moved away. Opening the door, he made sure to step out before Seth could come in. I could hear them talking, walking away, until their voices faded out.

I lowered myself to the ground, threaded my hands into my hair, and tugged as I groaned in frustration.

What the fuck was I supposed to do now?

# CHAPTER THIRTEEN

I allowed myself one minute. Sixty seconds to fall apart, wallow in the fear and the misery. I counted them out even as I hugged my knees to my chest and felt sorry for myself, wondering if Riley had chosen his brother over me, despairing about how everything was fucked.

When I got to sixty, I took a deep breath and forced myself to my feet.

Maybe Riley was helping his brother get away; maybe he was trying to protect me like he said. He'd left me with the video evidence, after all. He may have been having a hard time dealing with the constantly narrowing chance at saving his brother's soul, but he'd supported me through this all regardless.

But if he loved Seth as much as I loved Ben . . .

*Enough.*

I wiped my face and marched into the bedroom. I pulled on my black yoga pants, a black long-sleeved T-shirt of Riley's, and my sneakers. I grabbed my phone and Ben's and walked out the back door.

They were maybe five minutes ahead of me. It was long

enough that I couldn't see them but short enough that I wouldn't be far behind—if they were actually going to the hot shop.

I was taking the video to the police. I didn't care what anyone else said or thought. It was happening.

I was just going to make a little pit stop along the way.

If Riley had been lying, then I'd know when I got to the workshop. If he hadn't been lying, I'd . . . I didn't know. I'd only had a few minutes to make up my mind, so excuse me if the plan wasn't exactly fleshed out.

All I knew was that I was done doubting my instincts. And my instincts were telling me to follow them to the workshop. I'd work the rest out when I got there.

The beach was empty, the moon bright over the water as I marched across the sand. Even Pelly's wasn't as lively as usual.

Murder was bad for business, I guess.

The dark clothing made it easier to rush through the residential streets unseen, not that I'd come across many people anyway once I was past the main strip.

I was just a few blocks away from Ziggy's when the front door of a house I was walking past opened. My heart jumped into my throat, and I kept my head down, quickening my steps.

"Chloe?" Jess's voice made me turn around. She rushed to me, her eyes wide. "Girl, what is going *on*? I heard that someone washed up on the beach and you . . . um . . . people are saying you knew them or something? I've been at work all day, and I only just heard the news. I was on my way to see you."

She stopped rambling and pulled me into a hug. "Are you OK?"

I usually hated it when people asked that. How the fuck

were you supposed to answer? That question generally came up when someone noticed something was definitely *not* OK. But coming from Jess, it felt like genuine concern and care.

I hugged her back, holding on tight.

"It was my brother," I said against her shoulder, my voice breaking at the end.

*Shit, I do not have time to fall apart again.* I pulled away from her and tried to shake it off.

"Hey, it's OK." She took my hand. "Let it all out. I'm here. I am so, so sorry, Chloe. I can't even imagine."

"Thanks." I cleared my throat. "Listen, I'll tell you everything later, but I have to go do something."

I was already turning away.

"Wait!" She held on to my hand. "Do what? Do you need help?"

"I don't have time to explain. It has to do with my brother's murder, and I—"

"Murder!?" She bugged her eyes out. "Holy shit."

An idea struck me. I couldn't let her come along, but I could trust her to deliver something for me.

"You want to help?" I pulled Ben's phone out of my pocket and pressed it into her hands. "Take this to the police. Hand it over to the feds—not the local police, OK? Tell them to watch the first video on the camera roll, then tell them to come to Ziggy's workshop."

"OK." She frowned but took the phone.

"Jess, be loud. Do not take no for an answer. This is beyond serious."

"I got this." She nodded.

I couldn't wait any longer. With one last firm look, I took off. I could hear Jess running in the opposite direction.

The side door to the workshop was half-open, light

spilling out onto the cracked concrete. As quietly as I could, I sneaked up to the door, careful where I stepped and hyperaware of my surroundings. I could hear voices drifting out into the light, but I couldn't make out what they were saying.

Staying low, I slowly peeked around the doorjamb—a stack of boxes next to a staircase was blocking my view. I pushed the door open painfully slowly, dreading the moment it squeaked and gave me away. It didn't, and I was able to slip inside and move the several steps to crouch behind the boxes.

"What are you talking about?" Seth yelled, making me jump. Now that I was inside, I could hear when Riley responded in a normal volume.

"Seth, think about this. If you run, they will catch you, and then you're looking at real time. Like, the rest of your life kind of time. If you—"

"Turn myself in? Do not say that shit to me again, bro."

They were here. Riley had done exactly as he'd said he would. He'd gotten his brother away from me to protect me, and he'd brought him to the workshop. I didn't have time to feel the relief that coursed through me. I wasn't sure I could've handled it if Riley had betrayed me, abandoned me, broken me all over again.

I put one foot on the bottom step and peered around the boxes. Between the railing slats, I could see Riley and Seth standing by one of the furnaces. Ziggy wasn't anywhere in sight, but that wasn't unusual. He generally headed home not long after Riley got there.

"If you turn yourself in, tell them what really happened," Riley said, "they'll be lenient."

"And what if they're not, huh? Fucking pigs, they'll lock me away regardless of whether I did it or not. No. No, I need to go. I'll head to . . . um . . . I'll take the bike and ride up the coast . . . I'll . . ." He tugged at his hair, pacing back and forth.

That asshole was *not* getting away.

I prayed that Riley would keep him put until Jess got the police here. But I could do a little more to help them out too.

Taking a page from my big brother's book, I pulled my phone out. I kept it close to my chest so the light wouldn't draw attention as I unlocked it, opened the camera, and started filming.

If this fucker was going to run for it, I was going to get on video where he planned to go.

"Did you?" Riley's question made Seth stop pacing.

"Did I *what*?" He squared off with his brother, chest heaving.

"Did you kill the guy that washed up this morning?"

"What the fuck does it matter if I actually did it?"

"It matters to me."

"WHY?"

"He was Chloe's brother!" Riley shouted back. "Ben is Chloe's brother."

"Who the fuck is Chloe? And how do you know his name was Ben?"

"Seriously? You've met her several times. She's fucking living with me. Are you that self-absorbed?" Riley sounded equal parts astounded and frustrated.

"Wait, wait, wait. You're trying to get your own brother to go down for some *bitch*?" Seth shook his head. "What the fuck happened to you, bro?"

"I grew up. And don't you ever fucking talk like that about her again."

Seth shoved Riley in the chest. "She's just some chick.

Ben was just a bored rich kid who stuck his nose where it didn't belong. I am your *blood*. Your *family*."

"And Ben is Chloe's family," Riley shot back. "How do you think she feels right now? How do you think she felt seeing her brother wash up on the damn beach?"

"I don't give a flying fuck how she felt!" Seth smacked something off the workbench, and it clattered to the ground. He was getting more agitated.

"Who did it, Seth?" Riley pushed. "Who killed Ben?"

Seth went very still, staring into space for a few moments before taking a deep breath and standing up to his full height.

"I fucking did it. Choked the life out of him with my bare hands. And I'd do it again. He knew too much. And you know just as well as I do that if I hadn't, Dad would've, or any one of the other guys."

Tears poured down my cheeks, and I had to bite the inside of my mouth to stop myself from crying out loud. Ben must've been so scared. His last moments must've been horrific, filled with pain and violence and terror.

And this remorseless piece of shit was responsible.

"And you know what else?" Seth kept speaking. "I'm not fucking going down for it. I don't know what you're trying to do here, big bro, but it ain't helping me. I'm out of here."

He turned and started walking toward me and the door, but Riley grabbed his arm roughly and made him stop.

"The fuck you are."

Instead of answering, Seth leaned into the momentum of his turning body and punched Riley right in the jaw.

I gasped, almost dropping the phone, but they didn't hear me over the sounds of their fighting.

Riley threw a punch right back, and then they were really going at it.

They punched, kicked, and threw each other around viciously, bumping into benches and equipment. Glass shattered, metal tools made a racket on the concrete floor, and the brutal sound of skin smacking against skin filled the cavernous space.

They were pretty evenly matched. As brothers, they had the same build. They both kept fit. They both had violence in their pasts and knew how to do damage with their fists. It wasn't long until they were bloodied. Seth's lip was cut, Riley's nose was bleeding, and both their knuckles were red and swollen.

I chewed on my bottom lip, flinching every time Seth landed a punch.

They grappled, and Riley managed to get the upper hand. He got behind Seth and dunked his head into the barrel of water next to a workbench. My anxiety calmed the tiniest bit. All Riley had to do was keep Seth here until the police arrived. Surely any minute now. But I had no way of knowing if Jess had managed to convince them yet.

Seth flailed and knocked the barrel over. Water went everywhere.

With a guttural yell, full of frustration and rage, he slammed the back of his head into Riley's face. Riley stumbled backward, stunned, and Seth rounded on him.

He mercilessly laid into the man I loved, landing rapid punches to Riley's head and torso as Riley retreated as best he could.

Seth had killed my brother, and now he looked ready to kill his own.

I glanced over my shoulder at the door. Where the fuck were the police?

In the split second it had taken me to look at the door, Seth had backed Riley up next to one of the glory holes. He grabbed his head and started pushing it with all his might toward the hole radiating white heat.

Those things burned at over 2,500 degrees.

He was going to burn him alive.

He was actually going to kill him.

I dropped the phone, not caring if it was still recording or that it had clattered on the step. I just ran straight for the two extremely dangerous men in a life-or-death battle.

With one firm grip on Riley's head, Seth reached for the gun tucked into the back of his pants.

I grabbed the first thing I saw that could actually do some damage. There were several blowpipes lined up on the holder, two of them sitting under flames in preparation for gathering molten glass.

I gripped one firmly and swung it as hard as I could.

It connected with Seth's head, and he dropped the gun and released Riley while letting loose a horrifying scream.

I'd whacked him hard, with the hot end of a metal stick. The side of his head was burned.

He looked as if he was in so much pain he couldn't even see straight. His voice was getting hoarse from screaming,

I kept the blowpipe raised over my head, my arms burning with the weight of it, ready to swing again if Seth tried anything. Riley took a few moments to recover and backed away from the furnace, shaking his head as though to clear it. He was stumbling, dazed, but in better shape than his brother.

Seth's screaming settled down, and he ended up on the ground, lying on the side that wasn't burned.

I relaxed my grip on the metal pole and lowered it to my side. Riley was leaning on a bench, catching his breath.

In the distance, the wail of sirens cut through the night.

I walked over to Seth and bent down so I could look him in the eyes.

"That was for Riley." I gestured to his head, and he flinched away from me. "And this is for Ben."

Standing back up to my full height, I pressed the tip of the blowpipe to his cheek. Just for a moment. Just enough that it would leave an ugly mark on his cheek for the rest of his miserable life.

It matched the ugly mark on my soul, the gnarled place in my heart where Ben used to be.

He screamed, shuffling away, and then Riley was there with a gentle touch on my shoulder.

The sirens got louder.

I let the metal pole clatter to the ground and turned into Riley's embrace.

We held each other tightly until the police burst through the door.

# EPILOGUE

It was a beautiful day. The sky was blue, and the sun was bright, obscured only occasionally when a fluffy white cloud came floating past.

It was exactly the kind of day Ben deserved for his funeral.

The sun felt warm on my shoulders, but not the kind of hot I'd gotten used to in Verbena Cove. We were a long way from there.

Ben had wanted to come home—he'd told me in his last voicemail—and that's where he was brought.

The past few weeks had been the worst of my life. When the police showed up to Ziggy's, they arrested Seth, and over the next few days, they rounded up his father and the rest of the lowlifes they committed crimes with.

Riley and I were both interviewed extensively. Between our reports, Ben's video and voicemail, and my video, they had plenty to charge Seth with. And they had reason to dig into his associates. A lot of bad people were going away for a long time.

I just wished my brother hadn't had to die for it.

Riley took my hand as one of Ben's childhood friends finished delivering his eulogy. On my other side, my mother was sobbing. My dad held her around the shoulders, tears tracking down his cheeks too.

Calling to tell them about Ben had been one of the hardest things I'd ever done. They were beyond devastated, racked with guilt for not believing me, and making a genuine effort to be actual human beings for once.

I guess it was a start.

There were a lot of people standing on the gently sloping grass in front of the family plot. Ben was well-liked, and it warmed my heart to know I wasn't the only one who would truly mourn and miss him.

Mom and Dad had wanted to bury him, but I'd insisted he be cremated. I had a feeling he'd prefer it that way. The urn with his ashes sat on a plinth, a big picture of him next to it.

I'd insisted that we ban anyone from wearing black too. Ben was bright and full of love and laughter, and he would've hated to see everyone he knew standing around looking like an emo concert audience. The sight of all those people dressed in bright colors in honor of my big brother made it easier to breathe.

I took a deep breath into my lungs, tipping my head back to watch the leaves swaying in the breeze for just a few moments.

"You doing all right?" Riley whispered in my ear, his hand tightening around mine.

"No." I shook my head. "But I will be."

A lot of people wanted to say a few words, myself included, and then there was to be a wake at the function space in the middle of the cemetery. As everyone started to make their way there slowly, I decided I didn't want to go.

I didn't want to waste another moment.

Grabbing the urn, I turned to Riley. He saw my thoughts in my eyes, smiled, and held his hand out, ready to stay by my side as he had been since the first day I met him.

"Chloe?" My mom's watery voice made me turn. Dad was with her too. They both looked haggard. "Are you coming?"

"No, Mom, I'm not." I shook my head but gave her a gentle smile.

Disapproval creased her brow, but before she could lay down a guilt trip, Dad stepped around her and pulled me into a hug.

"I'm proud of you, Chloe," he said, his voice as shaky as Mom's. "And I love you. I never said that enough to Ben—or you. But I'm going to make sure you know."

"Thanks, Dad." I hiccupped.

He released me, and Mom took his place. She gave me a firm squeeze as we sobbed on each other's shoulders, Ben's ashes between us. "I love you so much, my sweet girl."

"I love you both too."

"You bring some of him back for me, OK?" She pulled away and patted the urn in my arms.

"I promise."

"Take care of my girl," Dad said to Riley.

"I'll protect her with my life." My gorgeous, loving man shook my dad's hand.

Mom and Dad headed to the wake, and Riley and I walked toward the parking lot. Our brand-new van was parked there, ready to take us to our future.

I'd quit college. Riley's parole was up months ago. We were getting into that van and driving to a beach. The plan was to explore the beaches and the countryside, the cities and the galleries. To learn new art techniques and maybe even how to surf. We were going to drive around the country and have an adventure.

Just as Ben had started to.

Just as I realized I wanted to.

I planned to sprinkle a bit of Ben's ashes on every beach we went to, making sure he got to come with me on the adventure he'd always dreamed of.

My brother and I were both free now, and I was going to live my life to the fullest for both of us.

THE END

***

Thank you for reading *Sand and Secrets*. I hope you enjoyed the mystery and angst of it all. And if you'd like to read another contemporary romance packed with secrets and longing, check out *Like You Care*. Mena and Turner's story is just as gut-wrenching! Read it for FREE in KU - https://geni.us/likeyoucare

I am nothing.

Nobody.

I'd rather be invisible than deal with what happens on the days my classmates decide to acknowledge my existence.

But then Turner Hall shows up - all cool confidence and witty banter - and all of a sudden I don't want to be invisible any more. I want to be seen.

I want him to see me.

I'm not who he thinks I am but I'm starting to suspect he's not all he says he is either.

Just my luck that he starts to make friends with my tormentors. How am I supposed to tell him who I really am? How am I supposed to show him my true face? What if the boy I'm falling in love with decides I'm nothing too?

One-click Like You Care now - https://geni.us/likeyoucare OR keep reading for a sneak peak at the first chapter!

# NOTE FROM THE AUTHOR

I really hope you enjoyed reading *Sand and Secrets* and you'll consider leaving a review.

Want exclusive access to advanced copies of all my books? If you're a blogger, bookstagrammer, booktoker, or reviewer, join my master list and never miss an ARC opportunity!

https://kaydencesnow.com/masterlist

# LIKE YOU CARE

## Prologue

The cable tie around my wrists was so tight my fingers were going numb. The pole they'd tied me to dug into my back, the cold metal and the evening breeze making me shiver.

Or maybe I was shivering from fear.

They'd never gone this far before, never hurt me this badly.I sobbed, the flood of tears stinging my sore cheek.

The knife was small--just a little switchblade thing--but it looked sharp. A shudder raced down my spine as the tip was dragged gently down my throat, the middle of my chest, my belly.

For the first time, I wondered if I would actually survive this night. Were they really about to kill me? Did their hatred really run that deep?

Movement in the distance caught my attention. Someone was sprinting toward us across the football field.

My heart soared . . . then I recognized him, and it plummeted again.He stopped just a few feet away, breathing hard, his wide eyes taking in the whole f**ked-up scene. He

couldn't hide his reaction; his beautiful face gave it all away-
-surprise, horror, disbelief, disgust . . . was that anger I saw
next?

I couldn't be sure of anything anymore. My soul was
being torn to shreds, and my mind was going with it. I had
no idea what he'd do next.

Would he join in and help them destroy me?

Would he stand by and do nothing, let it happen?

Would he walk away, like a coward, so he wouldn't have
to watch?Or would he defend me? Save me?

Knowing what I'd just learned, what it would mean,
what it would cost, did I even want him to?

He took a step forward, and I braced myself to find out
if the boy I loved would be my salvation . . . or if my heart
would be torn to shreds right along with my mind and soul.

Keep reading - https://geni.us/likeyoucare

# ABOUT THE AUTHOR

Kaydence Snow has lived all over the world but ended up settled in Melbourne, Australia. She lives near the beach with her husband.

She draws inspiration from her own overthinking, sometimes frightening imagination, and everything that makes life interesting: complicated relationships, new experiences and good food and coffee. Life is not worth living without good food and coffee!

She believes sarcasm is the highest form of wit and has the vocabulary of a highly educated, well-read sailor. When she's not writing, thinking about writing, planning when she can write next, or reading other people's writing, she loves to travel and learn new things.

To keep up to date with Kaydence's latest news and releases sign up to her newsletter here:

kaydencesnow.com/#newsletter

Join her reader group here:

facebook.com/groups/KaydenceSnowLodge

Or follow her on:

BY KAYDENCE SNOW

## The Evelyn Maynard Trilogy

Variant Lost

Vital Found

Vivid Avowed

The Complete Evelyn Maynard Trilogy

## Devilbend Dynasty

Like You Care

Like You Hurt

Like You Should

Like You Know

## Standalones

Reverie and Redemption

Just Be Her

It Started With a Sleigh